the
CROCODILES

the
CROCODILES

A NOVEL

YOUSSEF RAKHA

TRANSLATED FROM THE ARABIC BY ROBIN MOGER

SEVEN STORIES PRESS
New York

First published in 2013 in Arabic by Dar al-Saqi, Nour Building, Oueini Street, Verdun, Beruit, Lebanon.

First English-language edition published November 2014

Seven Stories Press
140 Watts Street
New York, NY 10013
www.sevenstories.com

College professors and high school and middle school teachers may order free examination copies of Seven Stories Press titles. To order, visit www.sevenstories.com/textbook or send a fax on school letterhead to (212) 226-1411.

Book design by Jon Gilbert

Library of Congress Cataloging-in-Publication Data

Rakha, Yusuf.
  [Tamasih. English]
  The crocodiles : a novel / Youssef Rakha ; [English translation by Robin Moger].
  -- Seven Stories Press first edition.
      pages cm
  ISBN 978-1-60980-571-5
  I. Moger, Robin, translator II. Title.
  PJ7960.A38T3513 2014
  892.7'37--dc23

                          2014005054

Printed in the United States

9 8 7 6 5 4 3 2 1

To Heba and Mohab

And they came to their father at eventide, weeping.

—SURAT YOUSSEF, 16

The Crocodiles' Cairo

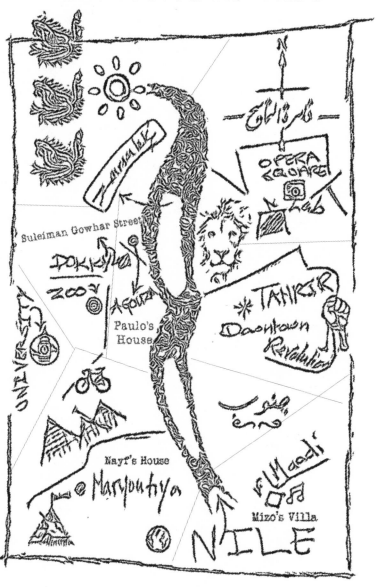

The Lion for Real
by Allen Ginsberg

"Soyez muette pour moi, Idole contemplative . . ."

I came home and found a lion in my living room
Rushed out on the fire escape screaming Lion! Lion!
Two stenographers pulled their brunette hair and banged the
    window shut
I hurried home to Paterson and stayed two days

Called up my old Reichian analyst
who'd kicked me out of therapy for smoking marijuana
'It's happened' I panted 'There's a Lion in my room'
'I'm afraid any discussion would have no value' he hung up.

I went to my old boyfriend we got drunk with his girlfriend
I kissed him and announced I had a lion with a mad gleam in my
    eye
We wound up fighting on the floor I bit his eyebrow & he kicked
    me out
I ended masturbating in his jeep parked in the street moaning
    'Lion.'

Found Joey my novelist friend and roared at him 'Lion!'
He looked at me interested and read me his spontaneous ignu
    high poetries
I listened for lions all I heard was Elephant Tiglon Hippogriff
    Unicorn Ants
But figured he really understood me when we made it in Ignaz
    Wisdom's bathroom.

But next day he sent me a leaf from his Smoky Mountain retreat
'I love you little Bo-Bo with your delicate golden lions
But there being no Self and No Bars therefore the Zoo of your
dear Father hath no Lion
You said your mother was made don't expect me to produce the
Monster for your Bridegroom.'

Confused dazed and exalted bethought me of real lion starved in
his stink in Harlem
Opened the door the room was filled with the bomb blast of his
anger
He roaring hungrily at the plaster walls but nobody could hear
him outside thru the window
My Eye caught the edge of the red neighbor apartment building
standing in deafening stillness

We gazed at each other his implacable yellow eye in the red halo
of fur
Waxed rheumy on my own but he stopped roaring and bared a
fang greeting.
I turned my back and cooked broccoli for supper on an iron gas
stove
boilt water and took a hot bath in the old tub under the sick
board.

He didn't eat me, tho I regretted him starving in my presence.
Next week he wasted away a sick rug full of bones wheaton hair
falling out
enraged and reddening eye as he lay aching huge hairy head on
his paws
by the egg-crate bookcase filled up with thin volumes of Plato, &
Buddha.

Sat by his side every night averting my eyes from his hungry
    motheaten face
stopped eating myself he got weaker and roared at night while I
    had nightmares
Eaten by lion in bookstore on Cosmic Campus, a lion myself
    starved by Professor Kandisky, dying in a lion's flophouse
    circus,
I woke up mornings the lion still added dying on the floor—
    'Terrible Presence!' I cried 'Eat me or die!'

It got up that afternoon—walked to the door with its paw on the
    wall to steady its trembling body
Let out a soul-rending creak from the bottomless roof of his
    mouth
thundering from my floor to heaven heavier than a volcano at
    night in Mexico
Pushed the door open and said in a gravelly voice "Not this time
    Baby—but I will be back again."

Lion that eats my mind now for a decade knowing only your
    hunger
Not the bliss of your satisfaction O roar of the Universe how am
    I chosen
In this life I have heard your promise I am ready to die I have
    served
Your starved and ancient Presence O Lord I wait in my room at
    your Mercy.

Paris, March 1958

[File:] The Crocodiles: Document 1 [2012],
The Lovers (1997-2001)

Anyway, these ideas or feelings or ramblings had their satisfactions. They turned the pain of others into memories of one's own. They turned pain, which is natural, enduring, and eternally triumphant, into personal memory, which is human, brief, and eternally elusive.

—ROBERTO BOLAÑO, *2666*

In their eyes, completed works conceal the incompleteness at their heart by way of an artificial unity: a unity whose purpose is to rescue their author. Incomplete works, however, are quite unashamed of this incompleteness. Indeed, they take it to its extreme as if to say, "You can never write alone."

—HAITHAM AL WARDANI, *The Incomplete Literature Group*

Among its peculiarities is that its voice slays crocodiles, that bile from the male looses what is bound and that its flesh cures paralysis. If a piece of its hide is placed in a wooden box, no woodworm or termite will approach it [. . .] It is of that class of animal that is reported to live for a thousand years and one proof of this is the plentiful dropping out of its teeth.

—SHIHAB AL DIN AL-ABSHIHI (1388–1446), *The Exquisite in Every Enchanting Art*

1. On the twenty-first birthday of a poet, ostensibly of our group, whom we knew as Nayf (his real name's not so very important)—on June 20, 1997, to be precise—the activist Radwa Adel went to visit a relative in one of Cairo's neighborhoods. I don't remember which. There is no documented account of this journey by the Student Movement's (or the Seventies Generation's) most celebrated female icon (i.e. the activist, though we might call her intellectual, writer, great thinker: they're all synonyms); there's even a dispute over whether the relative in question lived on the eleventh floor or the twelfth. But what I have picked up over the years, in casual conversation with close friends of hers from the circle out of which our group grew, is that Radwa Adel played with her relative's children for a little while, then took herself off for an afternoon nap in the bedroom with the balcony. There was nobody at home but the young children, and no sooner had the bedroom door swung back behind her than she went out onto the balcony and jumped over the wall.

2. Radwa Adel was forty-four. When I try to sketch out the details of her historic leap in my head, I imagine her sitting

on the balcony wall's wooden balustrade—why I imagine the balustrade to be made of wood, I don't know—dangling her legs from that dizzying height with her face turned to the street or the sky, while the children are in the living room unaware that at that very instant, Auntie Radwa's poised on the point of killing herself. I imagine her with her arms loose at her sides, then gripping the balustrade like an athlete on the parallel bars. Gradually, she starts to transfer her weight onto her hands and shimmy her buttocks down over the other side of the wood— bit by bit—and before they are fully suspended in the air she feels her whole weight in her arms. And she lifts her hands, holds out her unfurled palms like a person trying to stop something that's heading straight towards her, and shuts her eyes. That she died the instant she struck the asphalt is not disputed.

3. On the day of Nayf's twenty-first birthday, within hours of Radwa Adel's suicide and shortly after midnight, Secret Egyptian Poetry was born in Doqqi Square, and it seemed as though the working-class wedding whose din drowned out our voices in the café (likewise working-class) had been put on expressly to celebrate this event. The wedding was in Dayir Al Nahya, a short walk from the section of pavement we monopolized alongside the Al Sobki butcher's in Tahrir Street, and we were unable to see anything from where we sat. In the end, we didn't get up to take a look at the wedding, but the cawing cry, framed by the nauseating electronic jangling emanating from the loudspeaker, conveyed to us an ungovernable pleasure and, at the same time, further confirmation of our conviction that poetry, the thing we could believe was poetry, must needs be secret.

4. We had spent the previous six months endlessly discussing

how to define that thing: myself and Nayf and a third poet, who was obsessed with photography, and who, on the basis that his family name was Aboulleil, we'd come to call Paulo. To this day I don't know if Paulo's surname really was Aboulleil, but stranger still, I don't recall him having any other name. We were just younger than the poets who were starting to be published in *Grasshoppers* and *Counter-Literature*, and we would tell each other that those others—Emad Abou Saleh and Girgis Shukri, Baha Awad and Aliya Abdel Salaam (who wrote, in 1998: *Before God I will confess / That I am quick to weep, / That rulers are bastards and the poor an evil, / That love is a sickness / And people are devils writ small*)—that those others had come to the edge and had not jumped.

5. For reasons that will be returned to in a later paragraph, we decided to christen ourselves The Crocodiles, a group to champion what we dubbed Secret Poetry, and vowed between ourselves to write nothing else. This is the first sentence in the history of The Crocodiles Movement for Secret Egyptian Poetry.

6. Today—looking back on all this in the first days of January 2012; watching the outbreak of the second (or true) revolution on January 25—I don't think it unfair to restrict the rightful founders of Secret Poetry to just us three (even though the honor's valueless given the movement died out completely within four years), especially since, as a result of our philosophy, no one knew of our existence: we took a pledge from members that they would not tell others about us if they left. And though I've no doubt the pledge was broken every time, not enough people heard or cared about us for us to get a reputation or attract

attention. There were three or four enthusiastic poets with us in Doqqi the night the group was announced, and we later held an inaugural meeting at Nayf's family home in Al Maryoutiya that was attended by even more. But the others made no contribution towards the movement's beliefs and philosophy, and I doubt they bought the idea in its entirety. Ambition stood between them and conviction, just as it would stand between Paulo and Nargis, and as it had always stood between what we chose and what we wanted to choose.

7. Despite the dramatic rise in The Crocodiles' numbers in the months that followed, by the start of 1998, all that was left of those early members were one or two talentless poets. Under the influence of an artist with whom he was then in love, Paulo devised an equation governing the relationship between writing secret poetry and literary success in the traditional sense (literary success being, of course, an impossible dream at that period in Egypt, but one that, in one form or another, was still taken seriously within our circle). As for Nayf—coming into his own as a computer expert, acquiring an engineering degree from Cairo University, and translating American poetry from the 1950s—he kept returning to the idea of giving up writing altogether.

8. Throughout 1997 and 1998 we would go with Paulo to Opera Square, to a developing laboratory, behind a store run by an old photographer who had stopped using the lab years earlier. Paulo had been renting it at a reduced price since December 1996, and we'd smoke weed with him while he developed black-and-white films or packaged them after drying and, occasionally, as he printed pictures in the darkroom.

9. On the evening of June 23, 1997—aft[...]
on the way to Opera Square—Nayf v[...]
earshot of Paulo: "Remember the he[...]
Movement, Laith and Bahaa's girlfriend[...]
Hayawan and Bahaa Zayd.) Then, in ref[...]
lished book (and that, posthumously): "[...]
Premature?" And when I slowed and s[...]
pivoted smoothly without breaking stride and winked back at
me, a half-smile on his lips, his pace unchanged though now he
was walking backwards: "Radwa Aaaadel!" Then, in something
close to joy: "She threw herself off the balcony the day before
yesterday." "No, man." I'd have spoken in that classic Nineties'
blend of disbelief and indifference. "She's really dead?"

10. Truth be told, I can't remember how I reacted, save to say
that the topic never came up again, or never came to mind, for
the duration of that summer. Paulo, still angry from an argument with Nayf the day before the group was announced, had
turned to fix him with a look of revulsion as soon he began
to speak, but hearing the news he couldn't hold his detonating
snorts in check: "Crazy bitch! How did you find out?" And upon
Nayf telling him that he'd heard from Laith, who'd happened
to call him the morning before, Paulo reverted to throwing him
nasty looks. No one made the observation that Radwa Adel had
died the day the group was announced, and maybe no one had
noticed the synchronicity of the two events.

11. For Radwa Adel, the premature are those whose cycle begins
or ends before they are ready—as I remember it—like a newborn that has to be placed in an incubator or fruit picked green.
As regards The Crocodiles Group for Secret Poetry ending

had begun, it seems clear to me that something pro-
bound us to the activist or to her vision, although we
in't notice it at the time, or not immediately.

12. There's something in one of Wadih Saadeh's poems—I don't remember the context—about *a future that dangles down, for which the speaker spreads a net in the valley that it may arrive intact, or at least does so for its suitcase, the suitcase in which it sits and in which it arrives.* I know now that we never drew nets for our future, or its suitcase. We carried the suitcase carelessly, flinging it down to fall as it may. Maybe we thought of the future as too sublime a thing for its shape to be dictated by suit-cases, and so we did not acknowledge the end of The Crocodiles when it happened, and then, four years after that, our lives were visited by the supernatural.

13. We'd been six months talking when we announced the group. For a brief moment, in one of our sessions, I had the thought that our talk was all in vain because there was no writing behind it. The writing lay ahead, in the suitcase of the future, which only one of us carried and he unknowingly. Only one, who now must write to give meaning to our words all these years on.

14. It seems to me now—from my hypothetical vantage point in a future that dangled before us, unperceived, up until 2011—that the lion was the supreme secret: the lion that appeared to Nayf. With a clarity unavailable at the time, it seems to me that its appearance was not the only mythical event to have occurred. And though it was for sure the only clearly supernatural event, I myself never for an instant doubted the reality of the lion. Just that, with distance, I've become convinced that it was not

the only strange thing. Ghosts crouched atop our destinies all the while. At times they took the form of an idea or incident, just like the poem that comes from its author knows not where: vapors, risen from a vast number of life's liquids mixed all together without rhyme or reason, and distilled into one rich drop.

15. It seems to me, for example, that Moon—Nayf's lover, so-called because her family named her Qamar (which means "moon" after all), the first flush of their relationship not lasting more than a few months—was just the epitome of this tendency. And indeed, following the end of their affair, no one heard anything more about Moon or knew what had become of her, as though she'd come into existence solely for Nayf to fall in love with her: no sooner was he gone than she went up in smoke. Just as Paulo said of his lover (though she, despite emigrating, remained a turbulent presence in our lives): *"The dazzling embodiment of some mythical thing, which vanishes once the watcher is no more."* Viewed like this, Moon was purest poetry, and her ghost-like disappearance marked the final death of The Crocodiles.

16. Paulo: fair-skinned, irritable Paulo. The shape of his body varied according to one's angle of view despite the distinctive hump high up on his back (because Paulo's hump was negligible, it rather contributed to the uniformity of his outline than declared itself outright): now slender, now stocky. If he put on a little weight he looked shorter than he was.

17. The thing that leaps to mind when I think of Paulo, aside from his long brown hair, is the pale skin of his face, notice-

ably paler than ours. Though young in years his skin was leathery and as fibrous as palm fronds, an unfortunate impression exacerbated by his permanently budding beard and fitting nourishment for his ill temper, the rage frozen into the features even in his most placid moments. I'm aware that Paulo's face is before me now only because I saw it some months ago in Tahrir Square—the skin even thicker and more hardened, the body still transforming as the viewpoint changed, and all his hair gone and the beard turning white—but when I conjure up Paulo today, from my hypothetical vantage point, it's as though I'm seeing him as he was in the summer of 1997. I see him in the days of The Crocodiles and hear his deep voice, shot through with a scarce-felt peasant melody.

18. Fair Paulo and pretty Nayf. I remember nothing of how Nayf looked, only that he was more or less dark and tall and that his face, like his body, was glossy and divertingly harmonious. In my head, Nayf is associated with the ever-present bitterness in his voice, which with the passing years was to warp into a ruthless (though entertaining) scorn for those he talked to. His smile was ever-present, but you never knew if he was laughing with you or at you. His attitude towards misfortune in particular was dismissive, concealing a sorrow, or despair, or gloom: something profound and black, in any case. Aside from his voice and confident bearing, the thing I remember about Nayf was that extraordinary fluidity of his, maintained throughout his unceasing movement, and which—at the opposite extreme to Paulo—never once affected the way he looked, wherever he was positioned in relation to you. Nayf was beautiful, like the Prophet Youssef or a Greek god, and though not one of us ever grasped this, I believe his beauty was a prophecy of his tragic destiny.

19. A time will come when I, too, will argue with Nayf and each of us will curse the religion of the other's mother and hate him. And for all that, it saddens me today that I would not recognize him if I saw him by chance. That I might see him by chance is of course impossible, but the fact that I wouldn't recognize him saddens me all the same. In particular, it saddens me that I imagine one of us confronting the other with the revulsion of weary middle age and sneering, "Who are you, anyway?"

20. As for me, I'm no one. Youssef: anyone who lived with his family in Suleiman Gowhar Street back when the street was still a vegetable market; any Egyptian writer born in 1975 (or '73 or '76). Whatever the precise date, we were all born after the October War of 1973 and before the Iranian revolution.

21. To hell with names. Now, on the brink of forty, I've realized that all our names are borrowed, even those set down on our national number identity cards accompanied by (leaving aside the pictures, in which we appear simultaneously shocked and drugged) dates and places of birth, residential addresses, and religions. And like the other members of The Crocodiles Group for Secret Poetry—ever since the Internet and cyberworlds first appeared in our lives, then established themselves for keeps in the 2000s—there's no denying that I used different names in different situations and appeared to people with different faces in different chat windows.

22. Fair Paulo and pretty Nayf, I say . . . then me. "There is no me." (And as one of those mentors of ours, of whose existence we knew nothing until they were dead and gone, once wrote: "I am not I.") Or that I—other than the fact I'm talking now—

have no existence in the presence of my two friends. I am not, or rather: I am the shortest and coarsest-featured—known in our circle as Gear Knob, because the size of my head relative to my body is the exact ratio of a car's gear knob to its shaft—but I was also, perhaps, the most conscious of the creeds of Secret Poetry and thus the least ambitious of us all, or the most capable of following what was happening.

23. The three of us were a locked room fashioned from the scrutiny of poetry, or a life that resembles a poem: this is what matters. Today, looking back dispassionately, it seems to me that we really were the biggest crocodiles in the lake, the most vigorous predators of the small, uddered creatures who came down to drink, each taking his turn to chew them with a relish that knew no mercy.

24. Today, I'm convinced we were a room no one succeeded in entering except three lovers, and of them it's Moon who figures in memory or imagination though she was the last to reach us: Moon, the shade for whose sake we left a door ajar. As if the other two got in by mistake. Is it because we never knew where she came from or where she went after it all came to an end? Was it because of her tomboy traits and how they led us to covet this one woman above all others in our circle? Moon was closest to us in age and the only poet, after all. Perhaps on account of her hyper-insubstantiality and her possession—despite the slightness and small size—of a lion's charisma, perhaps because she was the most changeable and extreme, the one whose behavior it was impossible to predict from one day to the next, we left a door ajar for Moon.

25. In the evening I think on Moon as reports reach me from afar. Very far, it seems. Each time I'm made aware of the army's thuggery, then the lies of the military leadership and their political-media cheerleaders, each time I become conscious of people's readiness to credit lies, I'm ever happier with my remoteness. Here, I shall be cut off and secure: allowed to remember. It's truly pleasant to be spending my time tapping away with a clear head while Egypt burns, and I reflect that the problem—perhaps—is that it doesn't burn enough; that over there are those who talk about the threat the demonstrations pose to the "wheel of productivity" and the importance of getting the economy going even as young men are abducted and tortured; that people run for Parliament with claims that they "know God," while the scholars of Al Azhar's ancient seat of learning are slaughtered with live rounds. Because of this, because these events, in spite of everything, are limited, and because their significance is squandered on people's readiness to believe lies, I feel the necessity of remembering and am content with my remoteness.

26. In the evening I think on Moon as reports reach me and I'm thankful for the file before me on the computer screen as bit by bit it fills with words. I congratulate myself on creating a folder I called The Crocodiles—for this to be its first file—because, since doing so, I've lost the urge to descend to the battlefield of Tahrir Square or Qasr El Ainy Street and I feel no guilt. At times—and this is all there is—I am overwhelmed by distress. A biting light flares in my head, blinding and paralyzing me for minutes at a time, and I shake and awake to a severe pain in my stomach. An hour later—not a tear shed—comes a burning desire to weep. I know none of those who've been

killed personally, and though I've often put myself in the place of their family and friends—I know some of their friends—I don't believe I'm distressed on their account. The pain whose light bites into me is a symptom of something else, a thing I don't know how to formulate. As though you went to sleep in your comfortable home and woke to find yourself naked in the middle of the road. As though we have nothing else but this.

27. I think on Moon and remember that in December 2010 or January 2011, following the outbreak of Tunisia's protests—even as the Tunisian police were killing people in the streets—one of the loyalists of Zine Al Abedine Ben Ali's government appeared on Al Jazeera asking in a tone of disbelief, "Is the solution to burn the country? Is the solution to burn the country?" Now, a year on from the outbreak of protests in Egypt, I repeat his words in altered tones, his voice ringing in my ears as the reports reach me: Is the solution to burn the country?

28. And since I think on Moon . . . It seems to me, objectively, looking back, that she so engineered her life as to obtain the maximum possible quantum of love from the maximum possible number of people, even if the love—given that Moon was full of it and never made any real effort with anyone, that she was irredeemably so—was superficial and short-lived. We alone, and maybe two or three others, knew her well enough to love or hate her from the heart . . . But this is a tale for later.

29. In her craving for love bought cheap or at no cost at all, and in being—even her—married and quite ready to give her love to someone other than her husband, Moon was much like the other two; only, it seems to me that she surpassed them in one

essential respect. Perhaps she was too clever to take on trust the freely given, constantly fluctuating affection in our circle. Not that she stopped striving for this affection with wholehearted devotion for a single day, but I believe that she, unlike Saba and Nargis, realized it would never benefit her so long as she was not prepared to pay the price. Which is why she never appeared to convert it directly into an equation, in quite the same way.

30. Saba would gather people around her, by tootling an enticing tune on her trumpet, then exploit them on a daily basis to shore up her existence and sense of achievement. Nargis would reel them in by depicting herself as the victim of poverty, ugliness and backwardness over which she'd triumphed; she'd acquire people like artworks, piece by piece, then in her time of need brandish them like qualifications and titles in her doubters' faces ... But Moon would do something shrewder, immeasurably so. I don't know how to describe what it is Moon did, even after reviewing everything I know of her, but I believe it's intimately linked to ambiguity. The space for ambiguity with Moon—her vanishing and surfacing, her protean appearance, the importance she attached to secretarial work, more so, perhaps, than to her writing—the space for ambiguity with her was wider than anything else; it was what equipped her to find her ease in a closed room composed of us—myself and Nayf and Paulo—its walls constructed from the scrutiny of poetry.

31. Around the time The Crocodiles were founded, Moon's poems had begun to make a shy appearance in our circle. We conceded they were considerably better than the other poems written by women, but for all that, up until 2001 when she became part of our lives without our being conscious of the

change, we paid her no mind beyond a passing nod of admiration.

32. "Blood" (one of Moon's first poems): *Today, too, / the vivid red poppies / open inside clothes, / unseen by all but you, / and louder than the swish of speeding cars outside, / Edith Piaf's voice/ informing me that this pain's / your child I never bore. // Why does the music remind me that they're not roses, / that their purpose is to prettify the drug, / that they seem innocent while they are evil? // Every month, / with a joy greater than your anatomy can ever comprehend, / the deception pleases me, / as I moan until you pity my pain / that leaves me weak and craving, /and while you lick my tears, within me vicious laughter detonates / as I kill another / of your children.*

33. Now, it feels like Moon is fundamental and still present, so much so that I can't believe she had not yet appeared by the end of Millennium Eve; that at dawn on January 1, 2000—as we made our way back from that colossal concert on the Giza Plateau called "Twelve Dreams of the Sun"—life barely held a thing called Moon.

34. Millennium Eve. We leapt screaming from Nayf's speeding red Mazda as he pulled it in a tight circle, slamming on the brakes like a lunatic as it completed the turn. The car came to rest blocking half the road's width, more or less: doors open, music blaring from its speakers. We were teetering with our feet on the curb's lip, defying gravity, when a cat began to cross the half-span that remained into the path of a Hummer that was also, had to have been, returning from the party. We'd never seen a Hummer in our lives—this one must have been from

the first batch to reach Egypt—and its brutal size and shape only underlined our sympathy for the victim: a pale puss, the tousled fur that ringed its face lending it the look of a miniature lion . . . which fact preserved it in my mind, in memory. By chance the music hushed at the very instant of the Hummer's passing and the road was so still and quiet that we heard the bones crackle. The Hummer had been forced to slow down to avoid our vehicle, but no sooner through than it sped back up. It did not stop after running down the cat and most likely its driver was only ever aware of a bump or ridge.

35. We were utterly silent as one of our number returned, head bowed, having swayed over to where the small body lay almost totally flattened beside the pavement opposite, and reshaped, the cat morphed into a surrealist creature that Paulo would later term "The Asphalt Fish" in a poem. This Asphalt Fish: not one of us was brave enough to touch it. We never spoke of what happened; not then, not later. Just stood there, watching, as was our habit since becoming conscious of ourselves as poets; only this time, dumbstruck. I don't know if the cat's death had anything to do with it, or whether it was the effect of the pills we'd been gobbling without pause since the sun went down, but Nayf, when he got back to the driver's seat to straighten up the car, was sobbing with palpable anguish.

36. We watched the cat and discovered the grotesqueness of slow death as we would discover that the walls that made us a room, whether inhabited by lovers or not, were like drugs: purge them of the delusions that come with the first two hits and they're no good for anything—without delusions, friendship's a shared tone of voice and love's just interactive porn—and so we

had no just cause to run down the role delusion played in our lives. We were still green (though grown; though events were stripping our greenness from us) and I truly believe that we were delivered premature, so had no need of political events or concepts like "motherland" and "the people." In the period between The Crocodiles' announcement and that Jean Michel Jarre concert, with its silly mix of sound and light and seething hordes undeterred by either high ticket prices or the fact that the best areas were reserved for officials, I believe that the three of us were delivered premature, and Moon not yet in our lives. And perhaps it had to be so.

37. Even the Great Names of the Student Movement—so I assume, looking at them—may well have been destined for prematurity, whatever the incidents and ideas which shaped their lives, or seemed as if they did. I guess that The Twelve Dreams of the Sun marked the start of our understanding—we, The Crocodiles—of the meaning of life: a day in which the full scope of desire unfurled before us, out beyond the limits of the body's lusts. And we began to suspect that we'd been screwed.

38. In 1997 (and maybe afterwards) it had seemed as though The Crocodiles was the most important thing that had ever happened or would, so much so that we didn't give Radwa Adel's death a second thought. For all that, other important things were happening, not just in the world around us but also—and through this world—inside us. Transformations were happening to us. And perhaps the group's disbanding within a year of its announcement (practically speaking; though Paulo, Nayf and I would go on three more years acting as if it were still somehow extant)—perhaps its disbanding before it could leave a mark was one more piece of evi-

dence that it was not as important as we'd imagined, particularly in view of the fact that things were happening . . .

39. The following happened (to start with) about a year before Nayf's twenty-first birthday: Paulo fell in love with a married woman ten years or more his senior and was so smitten that he stuck with her, waiting for a divorce, for four years. Waited for a divorce or public acknowledgment of his existence, because divorce, as she started saying (about midway through the relationship), was inappropriate given the age of her young son. And as his attachment to her escalated he continued to be tormented by the assumption that they were together only to find out that she was somewhere else altogether. Time after time after time. Four years.

40. Paulo fell in love and began telling us about the one he loved and what he wanted for them both, which was baffling in itself, since Paulo, when it came to his emotions, was tight-lipped as it gets. He began to talk to me, or to Nayf, or to both of us together, with a quite uncharacteristic respect for the person he spoke of, ignoring our astonishment or laughter as he continued his tale: a respect or a regard, like admiration. His story didn't stop at the compact, burnished body, nor at the energy, which in his words was sufficient to power three whole literary eras; it didn't stop at his wetted lips and dry throat, nor at smiles of such purity that we could scarcely believe they came from him. He began to tell his tale and his telling did not stop at the gleam in his eyes that we did not take to be true tears until they had flowed freely in our presence at least the once, or twice. Their flowing was unprecedented, but it didn't annoy us or embarrass Paulo. At least, it didn't stop him talking.

41. Paulo began to tell his tale and it was a tale we'd heard before. Either that or we'd pictured it taking place so often that it seemed as though we'd heard it. Our enthusiasm for this story—leaving aside our delight that Paulo was talking at all—was like that of a screenwriter who sees scenes from the movie he's been toiling over for an eternity coming to life before his eyes. This is why we believed in it for six months, and maybe three months more. Nayf and I: we really believed the story and encouraged Paulo to live it. Until it came to seem that he was living it alone. It seemed at odds with what was happening in reality and so believing in it seemed meaningless. When we confronted Paulo with the fact that we no longer believed his story it went very hard with him, quite how hard became clear from the constant reformulations of this same story that he went on churning out for a further three years.

42. Of course, Paulo recast the story for his own sake even if it might have looked as though he were trying with each new version to convince us. But four years after their first meeting he would laugh along with us, from the heart, as he admitted that the heroine of his tale was using his versions of her story to promote her artistic endeavors, particularly now her own star had risen in our circle. As though he loved her for the sole purpose of becoming qualified to author a marketing strategy appropriate to a career whose decline was preordained.

43. This happened and it was without precedent, if not in our circle then certainly in our group, and I don't think we fully understood it, nor did Paulo himself understand, until 2001.

44. To prove to myself that up until that time we would embark on and end relationships quickly and lovelessly, I recall that when Paulo met this lover of his he had only just emerged from a month-long affair with a well-known rights activist in her mid-thirties or older: Saba. We all knew her at a distance, with her tall frame and wild brown hair, though Paulo's customary reticence ensured we never caught wind of their romance. I myself would have a much more involved relationship with Saba three years later, but wouldn't hear about her and my friend until the winter of 2007, four years before the mass movement—the uprising, revolution or protests of January 25; its names as varied as the viewpoint of the speaker—and it could be that Paulo sampled something with Saba that he could not let escape a second time, especially now that he had found it in a person (as he took to describing his new lover, and us believing him), who was—the person, I mean—herself a secret poem.

45. Not a week had passed since Paulo's separation from Saba, I'm saying, when he fell for a secret poem whose name was Nargis; well into her thirties at the time. None of us had heard of Nargis, though she was an avant-garde artist of talent. Her paintings expressed the crisis of the liberated woman who decides to live on her own in a closed society, and their fearlessness had been attracting interest for some years. But her name did not gain currency in our circle until she held a major exhibition in the Townhouse Gallery shortly after it opened in 1998, and for a couple of years after that Paulo would only be able to get her to himself two or three times.

46. It was around the start of 1996—a little before Paulo fell for Nargis—that Nayf first became interested in the movement

or school or craze that was the Beat Generation, the American generation of the 1950s, whose rebellion against society through drug taking, sexual experimentation and interminable talk, whose associating writing with an unorthodox existence in the company of down-and-outs and delinquents had much in common with Egypt's Nineties Generation, though they (the Beat Generation poets) acted with a courage and self-sufficiency that by and large was lacking in our circle. The leaders of our circle, as I recall, were less ready to risk or love and more susceptible to creature comforts, and the life reflected in their writing was trammeled by rules that went unacknowledged on the page.

47. The time that Paulo fell for Nargis marked the start of Nayf's interest in the Beatniks and, to be exact, in their most famous poet: Allen Ginsberg, the well-bred Jewish boy who never managed to sleep with a single woman in seventy years of stepping high and wide, all possibilities exhausted. He it was who would lead Nayf, over the course of four years and a quite incredible sequence of events, to Moon and then, through Moon, to the end of our tale. But the time for all that is yet to come.

48. As a result of being educated at the British School in Zamalek up until the end of his GSCEs at the age of sixteen (he sat his equally British A-level exams at the Manor House School to save on fees), plus his own affinity for reading, Nayf's English was better than any Egyptian I've met. And though, as he informed me, he loathed English poetry in general—even the moderns and contemporary stuff—an electric circuit came on in his head when a collection of Beatnik writing fell into his hands with poems by Gary Snyder, the street-child Gregory

Corso, Ginsberg's fellow inmate in the lunatic asylum, Carl Solomon, and Lawrence Ferlinghetti, who was the first to publish them all, along with extended extracts from Jack Kerouac's *On the Road* and *Junkie* and *Naked Lunch* by William Burroughs. Nayf told me that of all of them he loved Ginsberg best and that translating him into Arabic might be the perfect challenge for the Secret Egyptian Poet.

49. So it was that Nayf spent months reading everything he could find by Ginsberg, while Paulo fell in love with a secret poem whose name was Nargis. Nargis was a married woman ten years older than Paulo, and not a week had passed since his separation from Saba when he fell for her.

50. Nargis was an ambitious young woman who fled her village in Minya and married young to a well-known Leftist poet whom she left for a younger man, though he too was a Leftist and a poet, before disappearing for a few months to Syria or Greece (no one knew for certain and Nargis herself gave conflicting accounts). A year or two after her return she settled in Alexandria with a well-to-do engineer who had his doctorate from the States. She married him and bore him a boy. This engineer—whose name I remember, or imagine, to be Ashraf— had a passion for contemporary art and the company of artists, or for funding them, and had fallen secretly in love with Nargis when they met through friends, back in the days when she was studying at the College of Fine Arts in Zamalek at her first husband's expense, some six years before she returned from Syria, or Greece.

51. Nargis was an ambitious young woman who fled her village

but she rarely supported herself financially. No one took note of this last point, even though the assumption that she led an independent life was the key to our circle's respect for her and the favorable reception we gave her works, which, ever since the Townhouse exhibition, had drifted further and further from the atmosphere of courage and engagement in which, with persuasive adaptability, she'd initially managed to place them. Nargis was an ambitious young woman and I believe she really loved Paulo—there's no need to deny that she loved Paulo—but then Paulo really loved her, too. Madly.

52. Not a week had passed since Paulo's separation from Saba when he began to talk. A story we had heard or one that concerned us personally (and one that did not resemble the events narrated in the two paragraphs above, though neither did it contradict them exactly), however much we denied it afterwards or tried to play it down: the tale of a country girl who crosses a river of poverty and ignorance aboard a boat called culture and on the other bank discovers herself to be something beautiful. This crossing concerned us personally: the idea that culture (or writing, or ideas, or activism) could be a ferryboat; that a girl could cross over, or that she could become beautiful; that she could then discover herself to be so. How splendid the sails and oars . . . leave aside the fact one of us loved her.

53. Following the Townhouse exhibition—about a year and a half after Nayf and I began to doubt the truth of the tale he told—the beauty of this crossing would start to fade in the eyes of Paulo himself, who had complained of Nargis's appetite for networking and travel: her hunger to become a social celebrity within our circle at the expense of her time with him, to say

nothing of her family in Alexandria; her eye-catching ability to form relationships.

54. All this and the millennium had not yet come? Nor Moon?

55. With the possible exception of Ashraf, Nargis slept with no one but Paulo during the course of their affair, yet she never stopped contracting relationships. Given that she deliberately acted like a man, had done so since her adolescence in Minya (the only way to win freedoms like leaving the house on her own, sitting in some working-class coffee shop outside her village or returning home after dark; freedoms that would remain out of reach until she departed Minya in any case), a rule of hers—that she be a man or like one—that would continue to grant her credibility in our circle . . . Given that she did everything in her power to excite the envy of her female contemporaries and tirelessly fabricated controversies: gratuitous slanging matches entirely too vulgar to have any connection with creativity, though they served Nargis by establishing her presence and provoking her peers enough for them launch media campaigns against her, which made her feel important and controversial . . . Given that on top of all of this she sought the assistance of people who could set her up . . . Given this, Nargis's relationships remained limited to men, something that Paulo had no opportunity of objecting to since they, as she put it, were both adult and civilized.

56. To be precise, Paulo had no opportunity of objecting because Nargis would talk to him about her struggle. Her story was a story of struggle, too, and it was a banal story—something that would become clear only later—because it had been told dozens of times before; the story of nearly every female intellectual in

our circle who belonged to the Nineties Generation: from the petty despotism of a poor family to humiliation at the hands of employers in temp jobs and on the cultural scene (enthusiastic to get their hands on rare, ready-to-go goods at no cost); Nargis (naturally) never once benefited from nor inflamed their lechery —nor did she ever confuse accepting it with being free to exploit it. And as for those men of hers, striving to master her: Do you realize how hard it is for an independent woman to maintain a higher income than her husband while remaining a devoted wife (or divorcée) whom men don't dare approach? Do you realize how hard it is to pull that off and be creative at the same time? Huh? Do you have any idea? And so on until she made a name for herself in the circle and became—in the eyes of friends not overparticular about the truth—a consummate housewife and the genius of her generation.

57. Idealists are often less moral than non-idealists in the end, just as the pious are less faithful and the politicized less orthodox in their ideology. Similarly, romantics—I think—can be immeasurably harsher than others. Their romanticism's a veneer; deep down lies a scorn for life and a ruthlessness; a quite terrifying ruthlessness these romantics have.

58. I remember that Millennium Eve had not yet arrived when we were drawn to frizzy-haired Saba and Nargis with her chubby face. But the cat—this, after we had come to know them—did not die straightaway. Today, I reflect that our standing there, transfixed, supposedly listening to the music in the winter air as the cat passed away, let us know for the first time that we—just like the Seventies Generation and the Great Names of the Student Movement—that we, too, were premature.

59. We watched the cat as we would watch while friendship and love drove one of our number to wish harm on another, transposed from some delightful state that prompts a pair to walk in step into something hateful, that makes each avoid the other's path and keep a dagger cocked for him behind his back. There's nothing uglier than finding yourself wishing ill on a loved one or a friend, all thoughts of reconciliation and forgiveness useless because the cat's been crushed for good. You feel, in the moment, a longing for the one who was with you and yet, perversely, you lie or exact revenge. You feel, perhaps, that you're still searching fruitlessly for a vanished splendor in something grown ugly: vanished, or that never was at all perhaps—you dreamed it, then woke up. In any case you're compelled to admit that your salvation—the thing you figured would spare you your ambitions for a life of consequence, if not for actual achievement—was just something you dreamed before you woke.

60. Thus Nargis's desire to hold a place in the society of men, with no thought but to shine. And though her brilliance would always be dependent on the story Paulo had taught her to tell in endless reformulations, Paulo himself had no right to object to this desire.

61. Leaving aside her jealousy over Paulo (Nargis insisted that she wasn't a jealous woman, that she had never been jealous of anyone in her life, and yet her jealousy over Paulo was hysterical), his reservations over the virtual dick his lover swung from our circle's center to its margins were treated as backwardness and male tyranny. While the truth, as he once confessed to me himself as we sat up all night smoking hash in my family's apartment in Suleiman Gowhar Street close by Doqqi Square,

was that it hurt to see her squander time better spent with him on a social life essentially equivalent to her career, though she'd inform him, weeping, that she had never loved anyone in her life but him and would rather die than be apart. And neither sleeping with other women, kinder and more beautiful than Nargis, nor the readiness of some of them to consider him more seriously, could lessen the pain.

62. I believe our conversation took place in the winter of 1999. In the winter of 1999, Moroccan hash had started to appear and we were no longer forced to rely entirely on weed. I clearly remember that we were smoking some phenomenal blond hash during Paulo's confessional.

63. Nargis trembled in his arms, which proved to him that she loved him—so Paulo told me—but it hurt him that she kept him out of her public life because she was a wife and mother (while he was just a student at Al Azhar), though he had never seen her in her husband's presence nor ever heard of them being together out and about, other than at the opening of the Townhouse exhibition. He had the impression that her relationship with her son could be summarized as finding someone else to bear the burden when Ashraf couldn't make it and leaving him to Ashraf the rest of the time. To keep Paulo out of her life while she filled it with men she called her friends and whom she would unashamedly invite at five in the morning to the studio she rented by herself in Downtown, which it was in Ashraf's nature, or was his pleasure, to allow her: considerations of backwardness or civilization aside, this genuinely hurt Paulo, this use of her manliness to prove she was the smartest and most independent coupled with his desire that she be his alone—and a woman.

64. That night, after Paulo left, it occurred to me for the first time that one fact does not cancel out its opposite. That just as ignorance leads to problems which learning cannot necessarily solve, so there is a harm born of backwardness that lingers even after civilization has taken its place. That the harm continues to reproduce itself purely because that backwardness once existed.

65. My conversation with Paulo took place in 1999. In 2009—I would discover—he posted its contents beneath some random video on YouTube that had not the slightest connection to the subject: *Like someone filling bottles with air she talked to me of the absence of reference points: how they had gone from her mind. Nothing measured and none deserving. An ambitious girl in the city. To compensate for the village, cash bought sweating blood, and a substitute family of friends. Not one of whom provides for her though their intimacy oozes custody. And gradually, the city too becomes a village, the difference: that it has no reference points. I was always asking her why she clung to married life and one night, like someone bottling air, she told me that she'd cast off her crutches: there in the city, where places are traps and books dearer than songs, she will carry out her grand design alone. Before childbirth nudged her, hinting at the possibility of change, it would never occur to her that mingling blood might be a sign of equilibrium. She would gape, amazed, every few sentences. And it seemed to me that I'd move back and forth in memory according to how close I came to her place on the couch. Our meetings had become theatrical and baffling: the starting point open-ended. Yet not one of the villains would disappear, maybe because they weren't villains. Or was it that one fixation had been joined by another: that people can become bridges and that they can become obstacles, too? That's why she switched between her fellow travelers without it ever being clear just where their journey led;*

and through the stations the road remained too narrow for two to walk abreast.

66. In 1999 many things happened in tandem with Paulo's frustration at Nargis. And other than those literary developments that were to alter the rules that governed publishing and availability, we were not fully aware of what was happening to us—nor that we were growing up, suddenly—but we began to perceive how those within the substitute family, itself nestled inside Cairo's intellectual circle, were transforming into bridges over which their contemporaries might cross and settle nearer to the centers of wealth and power; how, too, these very individuals transformed into obstacles, blocking others on their way to those same centers. Behavior fated to be followed by demonization and charges of treason from the circle and, from society at large, by a shock and panic that reached its peak in 1999. Believing ourselves beset by the menaces of religion, tradition, and the secret police of State Security, we sympathized with those who did so, and viewed the bridges they left behind as something perfectly ordinary, something to be expected and quite distinct from the obstacles.

67. The obstacles were a necessary evil, in league with the status quo: so we saw it. As for one of us finding someone else, from another class or country, who might open a path to a new station in life, well, that was fine and legitimate; at least, it was less awful than staying put. Less of a failure. It occurs to me now that we were very fond of the word "evolution" though its only possible meaning in the circumstances in which we lived was social climbing. How did "evolution" live on in our vocabulary as some sine qua non that could be realized by unchecked leaps through the void?

68. And ten years after our story ends for good, I'll see. Just a few months ago, on October 9, 2011: I shall see clearly the reason for customs and traditions, wherefore for-shame and thou-shalt-not, and the cause, with these things as currency, of the trade in principles. Every time. Why is the only escape from such things to join a richer or more potent class? I shall see the endless talk, the strident tones that insist we're Egyptians or Arabs or Muslims or—within our circle—that we're none of these, and I shall see a lion cub fleeing for his life from his mother's mate, who comes to kill him on the sandy plains. Which is why everything seems like a counterfeit copy of what it's meant to be. Only in 2011—ten months after the eighteen-day strike that did away with the president of the republic, or his name, and before the outbreak of another set of protests against the army's leaders he'd tasked to rule before stepping down—only then, shall I see clearly: a terror-stricken invalid boasting of his lost health as, trembling, he snatches the hand of the person before him and stoops to kiss it, entreating succor. And I shall see that those tales of crossing are of necessity a lie, because there's nowhere for the ambitious to cross to; there's only climbing, until you occupy a place that lets you look down on others, on customs and traditions, on for-shame and thou-shalt-not, on endless claims that we are Arabs, or Muslims.

69. In 1999 things happened, among them the release of *The Matrix*. We watched it at the house of an American Arabist who owned a small cinema screen and projector; we watched it without drugs because, as this Arabist told us in his street-inflected cant, it was "a tab of a film"; a trip in itself. Honestly, *The Matrix* stunned us, more so than any film we'd seen, by giving

expression—through the fireworks and happy ending—to a profound idea that applied to our own lives, as we saw them.

70. *The Matrix* was a metaphor for what might happen to mankind in the wake of the New World Order and the Digital Revolution, but also for rebellion against the status quo: humanity's salvation in a revolutionary group working in the shadows. Everything we see and feel and do is a virtual reality streamed through our heads by a vast computer which has evolved out of human control and taken over Earth: our world is a wasteland; people lie in comas, their bodies from birth to death confined in pods coupled to the computer, their sole function to feed it and the machines under its command with the power they need to run, in exchange for a bare minimum of nutrition, injected automatically . . . Until, from the midst of the rebels who have managed to reclaim control of their physical bodies and realized what has befallen man, a savior arises, his coming prophesied years before.

71. In 1999 *The Matrix* stunned us, and the rules governing the publishing and availability of books were altered. From the start of the nineties something was changing—something that would lead, after the lion made its appearance, to the breakup of The Crocodiles, to our frustration, and to the revolution—something more than simply the transformation of Salafist Islam from a political project underground to a social obligation above it. Something was opening up the job market, making money circulate a little as the government raked in the returns of privatization. Fikry Ibrahim had brought in independent publishing with his Janoubiyat House imprint after returning from Norway in 1991, the same year that saw the first

issue of *Counter-Literature* released (in whose foreword Hani Foula wrote: "We look behind us, implacable and violent, and forge ahead with precision and determination. Make way!").

72. In 1999, dependent on authors' contributions for his funds, Fikry Ibrahim had set out to publish. Now, eight years on, a more vibrant climate had allowed Mahmoud Hisham to set up Serene House in Cairo and Bahaa Zayd to launch the magazine *Environments* in Alexandria—unlike William Wells, the Canadian who founded the Townhouse, neither resorted to the foreign funding that might queer his project's credibility or expose it to press campaigns—and the endless chatter of the nineties began to fade.

73. An unbridled force, never before sufficiently organized to be productive, was finding semi-secure and semi-legitimate footholds for itself. We'd choose not to notice that Mahmoud Hisham's publications, just like the limited runs released by Fikry Ibrahim, barely reached the bookshops; would note, derisively, that when the Islamists in Parliament whipped up scandals which led to books being confiscated they'd only ever target the Ministry of Culture's titles. But this vibrancy opened up new fields of play. An artist like Nargis now had spaces to exhibit outside the Ministry of Culture and its tame private galleries; now there were foreigners and wealthy collectors (and the dealers that hung around them) looking at her work and ready to propel her in directions that seemed progressive and evolved, that held out the promise of another tale of crossing, of transcending.

74. Gradually, Nargis would abandon oils and acrylics on

canvas and paper for installations and video; with time, Conceptual Art would lure her in. Viewed next to these new works, even her powerful early paintings would come to seem like stuff churned out to impress. I'm no art critic and I don't quite know how to explain, but with each new success, Nargis's work increasingly resembled the protest marches of organized labor, as opposed to the demonstrations for civic rights that sought to bring down the regime. As though the artist, whether through brains or malice or a bit of both, was anticipating the onlooker's response in order to give him what he wanted, reworked just enough to stir controversy, and with no thought to anything she might want to say to him. She created in order to prove something or to obtain something, I mean: not as an expression of her will.

75. You felt that Nargis painted things that resembled the story Paulo told and expended far greater effort in proving this was her story than she did in creating art. Thus she created, then lived her creation, regardless of what, deep down, she actually desired—the opposite of what we held true: that experience produces creativity; that a person first crosses or evolves, then becomes something beautiful. Nayf and I quickly realized that in this sense Nargis created in order to live, and did not live to create. And we realized that this would ruin everything.

76. Gradually, from 1999, these people started to appear who would live off funding from international organizations (which, save the support they supposedly gave to creativity, had nothing to offer), who'd take themselves off to organize such things in spaces that were fenced-off and segregated from wider society wherever they were in the world. So when creative types from

our circle fell in love with the promise these international projects held out it became easy for them to forget creativity itself—not to mention whatever ambitions they might have to spread this creativity beyond the circle's confines.

77. Following the Townhouse exhibition, Nargis would set up home in the studio by herself on a permanent basis. And when this happened (Paulo having graduated and gotten piecework as a photographer with *Al Ahram Weekly*) he would assume that they'd have more chances to meet and that now—now she'd achieved a degree of independence and he was no longer a student—she would be able to take the step she'd vowed to make since he first fucked her in Alexandria. That she'd divorce. Especially since her relationship with Ashraf was to all intents and purposes over before she met Paulo—as she'd assured him ever since he first fucked her, when it had seemed to him that all creation had fallen into place and found its order. Divorce was just a procedure, now that all creation had fallen into place.

78. We would learn that the boy shuttled between his father and maternal aunt and that Ashraf, despite his disgust at Nargis's absence and his anger over her affair with Paulo (when he found out), was still jealous of the unity and harmony of his little family. And we would learn that he remained fearful of her nervous breakdowns, usually accompanied by suicide attempts (attempts that were still life-threatening even if they weren't entirely serious). Only Nayf noticed that the artist Paulo loved, despite her words to him on deathless passion, was not prepared, for the sake of their being together one night or week or month, to sacrifice a single party or supper, let alone an exhibition in Napoli, Marseille or Barcelona or a lecture

in Austin, Texas, or a conference in Shebeen Al Qanatir . . . not even prepared to risk (any more than she had to) her husband's sympathy with an illness that, Nayf said, gave him the impression—and Ashraf, too—that Paulo was just another of its symptoms.

79. And I recall that Paulo himself, some fifteen years on—as we drank tea at the only café open during one brief break from the strike that stretched from January 28 to February 11, when Champollion Street was the place we'd flee to from the crowds and stress—would be swept back to the days of The Crocodiles on a wave of nostalgia, and drop hints that he'd not been wholly innocent himself: that Nargis, for him, had been as much a model of success as an embodiment of transcending; that he'd seen his connection with her as a chance to vault what he called stupid social barriers—something neither of us would have believed at the time even if Paulo had confessed it (and it could be he'd cooked up this motivation later, to lighten the burden of his defeat in love, though equally, this motivation might be true, somehow). With the possible exception of Nayf, we wanted, in some hidden part of ourselves, to use the girls we loved to vault the walls we thought we'd meet with on the way.

80. When people become bridges they also become obstacles. Those who cross over the ones they love, making for where they can see what they aspire to: they're the ones most likely to find in love the chains that check their progress or their rise, even when that love serves their immediate interests. Like the Marxist narrative of human history, their lives are fated to move forward in a straight line. Those who hate themselves for crossing over their loved ones only to find nothing on the other

side (or to be dissatisfied by what they find) are the first to bar the way to those behind them.

81. Now, from my hypothetical vantage point, I reflect that most of our friends who turned out like this did so for the very reason they first sought refuge in our circle: because they'd blown in from "behind the water buffalo" and they knew it. That most widespread of references to the contempt in which the country-side is held: "behind the buffalo." But the buffalo that bothers me is not the symbol of ignorance and poverty as is commonly intended. And nor is it, of course, determined by geography. I'm talking about low cunning and compromise; the cowardice that gathers men into groups even if the initial impetus comes from rebellion against the social mass. Herding together, I mean, or a life passed permanently beneath the gaze of people who are all alike. And all this despite the thousand complex forms their pride in their successes would take, successes that would seem, for all their distance from the countryside, to come entirely from behind the buffalo . . . our avatar. The buffalo that voids its bowels of muck to swamp us while we thrash arms until we bob up in the heart of Cairo. Ignorant or poor or otherwise, I suspect that, just as it stopped Nargis's story from being a thing of beauty those who loved her could believe in, it is the buffalo that stops people from being people, instead of obstacles or bridges.

82. Today, it astounds me that ten years later I'm yet to fix on answers to seemingly simple questions: Is it just that Nargis had a borderline personality; that Radwa Adel was bipolar (with the knowledge that her death had been achieved at the third attempt)? Was it Saba, perhaps, who tried killing herself

on more than one occasion before her marriage, after which that prey of chronic depression and endless replications of the same romantic blueprint stopped taking her medicine? Perhaps there's nothing more to any of this than an imbalance in the brain's chemicals. If so, then Nargis's behavior is evidence of nothing and maybe Ashraf was right to regard Paulo as a temporary symptom of chronic illness. In which case it becomes hard to fathom what beauty Ashraf continued to see in his wife, and with that, what truth continued to draw him into her story.

83. It astounds me that questions about Saba and Nargis still lie unanswered, but it is Moon who astounds me most of all. I swear I don't remember how I learned the specifics of her sex life with Nayf, but know them I do, in astonishing detail. I know the details of their affair though I never spied on them and Nayf rarely made reference to such things. Was it Moon who told me? Did I really sleep with her one lost night in the autumn of 2001? (If not, then how come I can see her naked in my mind so clear?) Did it happen while Nayf searched for her on the north coast? How could we have deceived him like that, even if we did so following my argument with him, after which I never saw him again?

84. I ask myself if the violence and physical torture in their relationship—that none of us understood at the time, not even them; that has taken on a mythic luster for me now—I wonder, I say, whether the torture and physical violence that ruled their romance had any connection to a supernatural event which I also know to be, alongside poetry that no one read, the prelude to a revolution that within months of starting would stand revealed as the echo of a cry in the void.

85. And I remember there was this one expression Moon and Nargis used incessantly, the pair of them: "It works for me." Not "I like it" or "It'll do," not "Fine" or "Sweet," not even "Perfect." No. "It works for me." As though the world were created for the sake of a fleeting fitness, determined by the speaker from her unassailable vantage point.

86. At a later stage Nayf would write, addressing his words to Moon: *"We shall caution the others to wait until the little creatures appear one by one, their udders swaying and snouts stretched out to drink. With no more warning than the dazzle of parted waters we'll rend the nearest in an eyeblink, the still pool turned cascades and our green hide in all its glory. But we shall suffer no jaw to approach, no single solitary jaw to approach us, my moon, until we've had the heart and lungs: only then shall we slouch off to the sunshine and there lie side by side."* Nayf would write these words for Moon and read them to us and yet—within two days or three, in the wake of some unplanned blowup in Zamalek—he would be back to screaming in her face: "The Crocodiles are bigger than you, anyway!"

87. Moon, who in the end refused to join The Crocodiles, gave the world not a single solitary poem from 1999 up until all news of her utterly ceased in 2001. Between 2007 and 2008 (so I heard) Paulo would search for her without success. As a poet who never published a book and whose work, to all intents and purposes, was only in circulation for three years, from 1996 to 1999, why then—and this is what confuses me—why then did she remain so obsessed with those who imitated her writing (from the writing of her contemporaries, the women in particular, she'd pick out the parts she thought they'd borrowed

from poetry in translation and state that, unlike them, what she wrote drew on no originals and was based on nothing)? Why so eager to prove that she imitated no one; that she stood alone? And then, if she knew the love that others in the circle gave was superficial while she was deep—I remain convinced, despite everything, that Moon was deep—how come that love continued to be enough? And if it wasn't, why strive for it?

88. Was it because she strove for something that would never be enough, that in the end Moon went away forever? I can't believe that not one of us ever saw her face again after the day Nayf asked me, following that drawn-out silence on the way to Opera Square, "Remember the heroine of the Student Movement, Gear Knob?"

89. The questions are unanswered and perhaps that's why I've come to be fixated on the story. But what set this document so rapidly in motion—it's time to let you know—is that I met with Maher Abdel Aziz after a long separation, about two months ago, while young men were being scarred for life on Mohammed Mahmoud Street, then outside Parliament and along Qasr Al Aini Street. The meeting took place close by where I'd been staying for the last four months or so: outside the bounds of anywhere that mattered. As though the place we met after all that time were outside the world; and for all that, as though Maher were meeting a person who was really present in that world, not some virtual voice sucking on the marrow of our reality from its place in a parallel dimension.

90. Suddenly he was approaching, his Nubian frame unchanged (Maher had abandoned every aspect of his Nubian identity aside

from his physical frame, and perhaps profounder things—language, culture—lay buried in unseen strata, swirled in with the mores of bohemian Downtown and affluent Maadi: no way of knowing what they were); nothing left but skin color, rounded features, the slenderness of his stock. A genuine affection illuminated his face despite the nerves that left him tensed and his eyes darting all over. And when we embraced, with the warmth of orphans returned to the refuge for the first time in years, and turned our backs on the empty restaurant to sip sparkling water and nibble crisp-bread, the writer who sometimes "committed poetry" (as he said of himself) seemed very old indeed but less melancholy than I remembered him.

91. That night, Maher settled back in his seat in front of me and in that way of his, which I found that I remembered well, he said—the words coming out in a sudden rush as though they'd only occurred to him that instant or as though he might take them back at any moment, and yet without disturbing the calm of his nonconfrontational, neutral tone—he said three things to me.

92. The first thing Maher said to me: That ever since he'd got to know me two decades ago, my head had been cracked in two; that though my mind might work, my awareness was crippled and that it was in the nature of such a constitution to ensure its owner remained alone. At a later stage in proceedings he added, by way of confession, that he was now of the view that the Nineties Generation had failed to move beyond the Seventies Generation in any essential regard and for this reason had played no direct, or even significant, role in the events of 2011. Had anyone thought they would? For this reason, too—so

I mused while he spoke on—the events of 2011 might not, in essence, affect anything either. When I informed Maher of my obsession with Radwa Adel's suicide he told me that the day after it happened—in the evening, at a Downtown café—he heard the news of the death of Wael Ragab, the young writer who'd returned home from a study trip to Paris after being diagnosed with cancer within months of his arrival in Europe. He said that Radwa Adel's death had come as a genuine shock, but that it had been subsumed by his sadness over Wael, though Wael was never a close friend.

93. "That's when things went to shit, I reckon," he said. "But why don't you write about what's obsessing you?" Then Maher added—abruptly, as was his habit: "You were far enough away to see clearly, but close enough to what was being said . . ."

94. Perhaps it's man's primal fear, still printed in his DNA, of being shredded by a pride of lionesses led by a male lion with its *libda*, the peasant's coarse felt cap that stands as synonym for the mane of the jungle republic's president (its military ruler), for the ruff around its face: the lion's roar begets a nausea whose like no call of beast nor machine din can match, no matter how loud or ugly; a nausea that's no less potent when great distances and obstacles stand between you and its source. Perhaps it's a primal fear of sounds that can only come from the throats of the four feline genera of Panthera, all of whom kill their prey with a single bite to the neck: suffocation occurring before blood loss can take effect. I had a fleeting vision of our unclothed ancestors bolting, hands clamped about their throats, as I learned that biologists themselves are uncertain about the mechanics behind a call so deep and powerful that it can be

heard kilometers away, whose utterance stirs storms. Some say it's the product of an unusually large parting in the hyoid bones of these particular cats, others that it's due to the length and composition of their throat walls. But I would continue to picture our ancestors out in the wastes and marvel at how the lion's roar is like no other sound.

95. In the winter of 1996, I was saying, while Paulo was falling for Nargis, the Beatniks had Nayf in their grip. Maybe it was only natural that he took Allen Ginsberg's death from liver cancer in April 1997 as a veiled directive to translate his works—Nayf had never heard of Sargon Boulos, let alone his superlative translations of Ginsberg—an impression confirmed by the passing of the greatest of the Beatnik writers, William Burroughs, some four months later. Nayf started with "Howl" followed by Ginsberg's elegy to his mother, "Kaddish." My view is that the translation was, for him, a necessary alternative to writing. It was, I think, a compensation for something whose pulse, for no clear reason, had been steadily fading away from the time The Crocodiles were founded, as well as a change from the work that left him increasingly numb in return for ever greater fees: Arabizing Microsoft and Adobe software for the new market.

96. In December 2000, months before he first met Moon, Nayf would begin translating his favorite Ginsberg poem, now that he had finished with "Howl and "Kaddish"—the two epics—plus a few assorted shorter verses. *I came home and found a lion in my living room / Rushed out on the back stairs screaming: Lion! Lion! / Two stenographers pulled their dark hair and banged the window shut / I hurried to the family home in Patterson and stayed two days // Called up my old Reichian analyst / Who'd kicked me out of therapy for*

smoking marijuana / "It's happened," I panted. "There's a Lion in my living room" / "I'm afraid there'd be no value in discussing this," and he hung up. A possible rendering of the first eight lines, faithful to the English original. But Nayf couldn't decide between this and a less literal version that seemed to him more fluent and closer to the life he lived in Cairo. *I came home to find a lion in the front room / And I ran to the stairwell screaming: There's a lion! / My neighbor the secretary gathered up her hair and slammed the stairwell window / I traveled to my people in the country and stayed two days // Spoke to my psychologist who combined Marx and Freud / And who'd stopped our sessions when he found out that I smoked / Panting I said, "I just found a lion in the front room," / But he said, "You've got nothing to say to me," and hung up.*

97. So it was that Nayf began translating "The Lion for Real" in two quite different ways, four years after The Crocodiles' announcement. But in the course of those years, things more important than the group's announcement were happening.

98. One year before Nayf's twenty-first birthday—and this was the first piece of information to show me that the synchronicity of the activist's death and the rise of secret poetry was more than mere coincidence—the following had also happened: Radwa Adel called Mojab Harb, the man she'd divorced a few months earlier and the last person she contacted before her suicide, pleading for help. None of us knew Mojab well, not as a Nineties poet from the Alexandrian group that had first emerged in the 1980s—Bahaa Zayd and Laith Al Hayawan in particular had a strong influence on the Nineties Generation, regardless of that generation's denials—nor as the husband of a Seventies activist some ten years or more his senior.

99. None of us knew Mojab well even though he was—as would become clear (despite the fact that he was a few years older than us)—the one true thread that bound The Crocodiles to Radwa Adel. There was a group from Tanta, too—Mohammed Mazrouei, Adel Esmat, Hosni Hassan and others—as well as a much larger one from Daqhaliya and yet another from Desouq. Certain neighborhoods in Cairo (Faisal for example) had groups of their own. But we never paid the place that people came from any mind nor dreamt that it might have any influence, especially since that in more or less every case the trail led back to the countryside, albeit a generation or two back at times. Occasionally I ask myself if I was wrong about that, as well; whether I'd been better advised to take account of origins when weighing up the destinies of my fellow travelers.

100. In the nineties, Radwa Adel turned on the group of activists to which she had belonged since the late sixties and with whom she'd held student sit-ins against Sadat in 1972, followed five years later by the Bread Intifada, the uprising triggered by lowering state subsidies on loaves. This, I gathered in passing from friends in our circle, among them Bahaa Zayd, Mojab himself (not to mention the first husband she'd met while they were both students at Cairo University, then separated from a year into their marriage), and the famous translator, Ahmed Hassan Al Jentil. She did not completely renounce her Marxist credo following the fall of the Berlin Wall in 1989, but one after the other she launched attacks against all the leaders of the so-called Third Communist Movement, especially the Labor Party, especially those who could boast a "leadership role"—their term for high-ranking status within the secret organizations.

101. One after the other she attacked them, those characters straight from the pages of Dostoyevsky's novels—and Radwa among them: Prince Myshkin or Alyosha. She attacked their social ambition, their hunger for power, their cold-blooded readiness to hurt one another in defense of theories that masked selfish dreams. All run-of-the-mill stuff, perhaps. But she also attacked them for taking refuge in the notion that they were outsiders; for taking the idea that the security services were on their trail and using it to establish themselves as victims of a tyranny and authoritarianism harsher and more brutal than that found in Reactionary Society (their term for post-Nasser Egypt). Nor did these poor party members have any way out, for they had nowhere to turn but the Party: no family, no jobs; in many cases, no fixed abode. (Did this happen all over again with us, a social pretext in place of the political: the notion of an alternative community in which taboos were smashed and the hollowness of a whoreson culture exposed?)

102. She confronted them with it, wrote it down, and was done, only to go back and write it down all over again.

103. And, just like another communist suicide by the name of Seham Sabri, though she turned her back on the activist group and went to work for *The World Today*, a newspaper abominated for its Gulf backers, Radwa Adel was unable to escape the concept of the group. I don't recall which friend it was that told me: "The emptiness was eating at her soul." For years she tried things out. She traveled to Spain and worked as a waitress in Hurghada, and other than the first draft of *The Premature*, which she completed, then destroyed during a bout of depression in Andalusia, I don't believe she set pen to paper.

104. It was the glamour of belonging to a set of younger people in new places. That their names had weight within the circle, without them being politicized, astonished her. She was drawn to what they said of themselves, or what was said of them: that they lived as individuals, as she'd resolved to live after the Communist Movement committed suicide. And it was in thrall to that glamour, as I understand it, that she followed the fad of traveling to Alexandria. The fad first surfaced in the circle in 1991. And because Bahaa Zayd and Laith Al Hayawan were there, gatherings formed around them from which those who'd later become The Crocodiles would keep aloof, though not unaware. When you asked the Nineties poet you'd bumped into at the café—and who, like everyone else, was out of work and writing nothing—"What are you up to these days?" he'd sigh and say in the tone of one embarking on some desperate adventure: "Going to Alexandria!"

105. New Year's 1993: I no longer remember how I spent the night. Neither Nayf nor Paulo were with me, though we were all in Cairo, and I was yet to witness the frenzy of spraying water and hurling old possessions from the windows that possessed Alexandria's inhabitants at midnight on the last night of the year. A custom that persisted for a few years until it finally died out at the exact same time as the bombing of the Two Saints Church on New Year's Eve 2011, twenty-five days before the mass movement swept loose on January 25. In 1993—Mojab would inform me—Radwa Adel was there.

106. How Mojab's first encounter with Radwa went, I've no idea. On New Year's Eve 1993 the greatest gathering of the Nineties Generation took place amidst booze and broken glass and drifts of seed hulls, hammering on more than one front

door and a friend behind each one: the painter Ali Ashour, the director Islam Al Azazi, the writer Abdel Aziz Al Sebaei and all the other Alexandrians. And so it was that Radwa Adel found herself floating in a quite unfamiliar soup: the stock was poured in and she went nicely with the veg. And it seemed to her, as I understand it, that she went especially nicely with Mojab.

107. From Mojab I would learn that they hardly spoke that night—their story wouldn't start for another six weeks, after they'd reconnected in Cairo and then again in Alexandria—but I still picture them, a distant dot on the Corniche as the sun rises over the first day of 1993.

108. As though I'm looking down on them from the summit of Saad Zaghloul's statue in Mahattat Al Ramal, sozzled friends asleep or singing at the windows: no more than a distant dot making for the fort on the other side of the bay. In a subsequent soul-baring session, Radwa would tell Mojab she had dreamt that he would give her a year of his life. Just one year. (Radwa Adel would take no more than a year of Mojab Harb's life, ironically.) "When we went down to the sea I was ready to carry her on my shoulders." So Mojab told me. "Everything was decided in an instant."

109. I don't know how their first encounter went. Mojab told me about another night that brought them together, one I think Bahaa once mentioned in some other context. There are nights, New Year's 1993 for instance, that are like milestones marking off the nineties.

110. That second night, the whole horde was gathered, accompanied by Lebanese prose poet Abbas Beidoun, at the home

of Abdel Razeq Shabaan: the Seventies poet who would produce, along with Ali Dawoud and Effat Yassin—who'd later
sign up to the Nineties Generation, body and soul—the *Tones*
magazine (while Hussein Al Bouhi, Ahdi Kamel and Khairat
Fattah belonged to the *Illumination '77* Group, named for the
magazine). Talk back then was still plentiful and forceful, so he
informed me: there was no distinction drawn between criticism
and destruction. Talk of poetry, that is.

111. According to both Bahaa and Mojab, Abdel Razeq Shabaan
spent that night trying to extract a confession from Abbas Beidoun that the new generation, Bahaa and Laith's generation,
the generation of Girgis Shukri and Emad Abou Saleh, whose
written language was drawn from the streets and its images
from the things they found there, and that had begun to make
its presence powerfully felt in the circle ... Anyway, according
to Bahaa and Mojab, Abdel Razeq Shabaan kept trying to get
Abbas to admit that this generation had produced nothing and
promised nothing. And with great guile, so I was informed,
Abbas refused to give him the satisfaction.

112. In October 2010, for no clear reason, Abdel Razeq Shabaan
would write about the wedding of Mojab and Radwa ("the
pure, dear heart," to use his phrase), voicing his disgust at "the
young groom" as he called Mojab—"as though he was afraid
to recognize the marriage; as though he were scared of family
and friends"—and expressing, despite this, a convincing sympathy for Radwa, a sympathy that seemed quite genuine for all
that he laid bare their private relationships and interpreted her
behavior with the mind-set of a coffee-shop gossip.

113. Reading that article now, it seems to me that Abdel Razeq Shabaan picked up on something authentic in her character—"It was as though she were embarrassed or put out"—and in doing so managed to locate Radwa's position relative to the broad mass of women's writing. Yet it also seems to me that he set himself at the selfsame distance, not only from women's writing, but from all the writing in the world, though he was not a woman, nor political, nor a suicide, nor married to Mojab . . . And despite his evident malice he says nothing about himself. Ignoring the assumption that Radwa, whether as a woman or intellectual, belonged exclusively to the Seventies and its corollary, that comparing her to the Nineties Generation constituted an offense against her identity, it was as though Abdel Razeq wrote to say, "I am Radwa," or "I am the activist"; as though being from her generation were sufficient justification for the claim.

114. Radwa Adel didn't attend the session with Abbas Beidoun in 1993, but she got word to Mojab that she was waiting for him at her place. So he left Abdel Razeq Shabaan's and headed over and had barely sat down before she handed him a penciled note, in which she talked to him about herself. The first letter. He read it while she made them tea, still unaware she was attracted to him. Eighteen years on from this night, in Medinat Al Sahafiyeen, not far from Mohandiseen where I'd pass most of my evenings in 2010, I pictured Mojab's eyes welling as he sat there in Kuwait, before a computer screen just like the one before me now, while his fingers tapped the keys to tell me he hadn't the self-confidence to believe that Radwa falling in love with him was possible.

115. It occurs to me now that Nayf and Paulo and I all met at one end of a rickety wooden plank which stretched from the mid-point of the century to its end, from 1952 to 2001, and that we stayed together until the plank broke. It seems to me that Mojab and Radwa met in roughly the same spot, though they parted before the break came.

116. Something took place in the fifties, something in history, which surfaced in the writing of the sixties, perhaps. And perhaps something in the writing of the nineties—supernaturally and incredibly, with a mythical indirectness—would contribute to the genesis of another history some fifty years on from the Free Officers' coup of 1952. But, starting with America's occupation or liberation of Iraq in 2003, and passing through the blow that shook the plank—in two installments—with the emergence of the Islamic state in Iran in 1979 followed by the collapse of the Soviet Empire in Eastern Europe and Central Asia in the early nineties, all the way through to its eventual sundering on September 11 in New York ... for all this time the plank on which myself and Nayf and Paulo met was always rocking. I don't think it too wide of the mark to say that the seventies were an appendix to the sixties, and the eighties a preamble to the nineties, even when it came to poetry.

117. When the first issue of *Counter-Literature* came out in 1993, Ahmed Abdel Hadi Tohami was the circle's sole surviving writer from the sixties, with the exception of Mohammed Afifi Matar, who, holding fast to Arab nationalism, had gone to the extreme of defending Saddam Hussein during the Gulf War. He—Tohami—had been appointed editor-in-chief of *Creation* magazine, put out by the Ministry of Culture, and had made

Hussein Al Bouhi managing editor. Starting with an editorial entitled "The Elite and the Rabble," the great poet would proceed—as it were, sketching out the front lines of the savagest civil war ever witnessed in Cairo's intellectual circles—to badmouth and execrate the new poetry because it followed no established poetical structure and because writing poetry that didn't scan was an abomination.

118. "The poet Abdel Hadi Tohami was right to openly admit his magazine is for the elites and not the rabble"—so wrote Hani Foula in his introduction to the very issue of *Counter-Literature* that Foula had led with a study of the religiosity of Cairo's street rabble, as if to spite Tohami—"because he has provided us with ammunition to prove the unfitness and moreover the corruption of those who stand atop Cairo's cultural pulpits." He published poems of the sort that displeased Tohami because they paid no heed to the fifteen poetic meters codified by Al Khalil in the eighth century, nor even to the conventions of free verse—or as it was known in Cairo, "foot" verse—which Badr Shaker Al Sayab and Nazek Al Malaika had cooked up in the forties by breaking up the traditional columnar layout, mixing structures or abolishing rhyme, before it was taken up by the broad mass of poets.

119. The battle over Tohami's prohibition on writing nonformal poetry would rage for years, despite the fact that the prose poem in its current form had been written, and favorably received, since the thirties.

120. Today, it seems strange to me that the Nineties Generation even engaged with this prohibition in the first place, that they

ever attempted to clear themselves of the charge—I reckon they did so to exploit it, to give the impression that when they wrote prose they were doing what had never been done before—but it seems strange to me because I do not believe that Tohami's words differ in any essential respect from the Seventies Generation's ruthless exposure of people's private lives, not to mention their poetry. And though Al Bouhi, as Tohami's right-hand man, was to become one of the symbols of government corruption in a way that others like Abdel Razeq Shabaan avoided, I don't believe the Seventies poets would have been capable of embracing any kind of difference (real or perceived), a problem exacerbated by the fact that the Nineties Generation themselves—just like any group, perhaps—included among their number (were mostly, maybe) idiots savants more than prepared to plagiarize, and virtuoso swindlers.

121. In the nineties a generation was taking shape. And for the first time in our literary history, it seems to me, the previous generation was defending, not a status quo against intruders, but a wasteland that, with nationalism and Marxism in retreat before capitalism and religion, the fading stars of the sixties had bequeathed them. And once they had embraced the theories of Adonis—in which poetry has no audience and modernism means viewing society from on high, or from some point further down the path of progress—the Seventies Generation found themselves defending, not an existence that concerned them personally, but rather a complex brand of nihilism, in poetry and politics alike: the Nineties Generation had either to become irrelevant—and politically they really were irrelevant—or be utterly crushed.

122. But Radwa Adel had turned on the activists, that's what I was saying: While Paulo developed his Kodak T-Max 400 films (exposed inside the original Leica M4 he'd acquired by some miracle back in 1995), while he fixed and washed them in a room no larger than two meters squared in Opera Square, Radwa Adel turned on her group. It was her habit to send a handwritten letter to anyone who angered her, summarizing— from a standpoint that might seem petty but that for her cast light on the personality of the friend in question—his lack of scruples and human weakness (there was consensus in our circle that strength was vitally important, though no one offered a precise definition of the term, nor distinguished between it and thuggery), or otherwise presented evidence of his failure to live up to billing as another Superman soaring through the skies of Transformation. Writing letters was a mode of communication Radwa Adel never gave up (even after she abandoned her political work for good), not with her friends (Laith; Al Jentil; Alaa Shukrallah, the human rights activist) and not with her husband, Mojab.

123. He informed me that in this, she gave evidence of exceptional intelligence and an ability to pinpoint weaknesses that allowed her to bring down the target with her first shot (arguably something she would do to herself, too). At all times she was after that repellent contradiction between words and deeds, making her something of an expert in character assassination— an expertise that some of the Nineties Generation would inherit (and not a single member of the circle, setting aside the degree of expertise or skill deployed, was innocent of attempting these hit jobs on those around him).

124. Now, from my hypothetical vantage point in a future that dangled before us unperceived as Radwa Adel circled about herself in her apartment thinking of an alternative to taking her own life, I see Paulo alone in the darkroom printing the picture it would have been better we'd never seen: the jewel; the prize . . . I see him pick it from the eleven negatives on the strip stretched out atop the light box. He slices two strips, five images in one, six in the second, and fixes the frame he's chosen in the enlarger's film carrier, set at the right distance for the paper's size. Just as I used to do, concealing the joint's coal with my hand as I pass it to Nayf—the pair of us squeezed in between enlarger and window—for him to take a drag or two until Paulo's hand came free that Nayf might hand it on to him in turn, I watch.

125. Weed in the evening, by red light, to the traffic's muffled roar, has a fantastical effect. And like I'm back there, the high trickling from head to nape against a fog of acids—while Radwa Adel leaves the apartment heading off in search of an escape she would not find—I watch Paulo switch on the enlarger to see the blown-up image on the wooden work surface, check that the lens is clean, study the balance of black and white within the frame, then, switching on the red lamp, douse the main lights and let down the curtains. A quick inhalation with his back to the enlarger followed by a settling sigh and, setting the timer for the prescribed count, he lets the enlarger's light fall onto a sheet of paper extracted in the dark and set in the exact spot on the surface he'd determined by shining the blown-up negative onto it.

126. And as I ponder Radwa Adel turning on the activists, it's as though I'm following pieces of cardboard snipped to different

sizes flashing like lightning across a sheet of photographic paper, set in motion by thin wires manipulated by Paulo's hands, and once again I imagine that I know exactly how many milligrams of light he must hold back from the light sections of the negative image to ensure they come out no darker on the page than he intends—as if the light were shimmering sand loosed from the paper to land in my cupped hands, its precise weight registering spontaneously in my head as it gathers—and as the timer sounds I see Paulo dipping the paper in the developer to reveal the compelling secret it would have been better that we two had never seen, nor any man besides; and he does not check it as he should until he's switched on the lights, the paper first dipped, after rinsing, in fixer.

127. And it occurs to me now, from my hypothetical vantage point, that Paulo, as he seals up the two strips of negative and starts to rinse the photo before hanging it to dry—as emotional and conflicted as Nayf would be translating the poem—that Paulo was in fact summoning up the lion. I don't think Paulo perceived the truth of what he was doing in our absence, nor that the photograph was no less than the first manifestation of the story's most dangerous secret: the supernatural thing; the thing without explanation.

128. The lion is the largest of the cats after the striped tiger and the only one whose male displays a ruff or mane, something that has led various cultures to prefer it as a symbol of courage and power over the other three: the leopard, the jaguar and the tiger. It is because of his mane that the lion is associated with royal bloodlines and the arms of noble families, and because he is lord of all the beasts with the exception of the elephant.

I learned that he spends most of his day asleep or dozing and patrolling the territory occupied by his pride. He makes no bones about killing the hyenas who covet his feasts, even when there's no feast to be had: to set an example. When mating—in sessions that might last as long as six days straight—he copulates with his consort every twenty minutes. He grips her by the neck, the same way he brings down galloping prey, ready for her violent reaction in the instant that he ejaculates.

129. In a subsequent attempt, Nayf would experiment with combining the two initial renderings without regard for line breaks: *I'd come home to find a lion in the hall and hurried to the service stairs crying out, "Lion! Lion!" at which two secretaries tied back their dark hair and with a clap their window slammed. I'd retraced my steps to my childhood home in Paterson and holed up there for two days. I called my witch doctor, a student of Reichian analysis, the one who'd banned me from therapy sessions as a punishment for smoking marijuana. "It's happened," I gasped in his ear: "There's a lion in the hall." But, "Sorry," he said, "there's no point talking," and he wasted no time in ending the call . . .* And so Nayf would proceed, aware now that he was in the process of creating a third translation: *I'd gone to my ex-lover and we got drunk with his girl. I kissed him saying, "I've got a lion . . ." the glint of madness in my eye. We wound up fighting on the floor. I bit his eyebrow and he kicked me out. I ended up masturbating in his jeep parked in the street, moaning, "Lion!" I bumped into my novelist friend Joey and roared, "Lion!" in his face. He peered at me, interested, and read me his spontaneous high-flown poetries. Ones written in the ignu style. The ignu's a person who lives once and for eternity and at night he lays down his head to rest in other men's homes. I kept my ears open, waiting to catch the word Lion, but all I heard was Elephant;*

Tiglon, offspring of lioness and tiger; Hippogriff, mythical monster; Unicorn; Ants. I didn't see he'd understood me till we fucked in the bathroom of a friend called Ignaz Wisdom, but the next day he sent me a note from his lonely desk in the Smoky Mountains: "I love you, little one; you and your dreamy golden lions. But since there's neither soul nor veil, then your dear father's zoo can have no lion. You told me that your mother's mad so don't expect me to produce a terrifying creature to be your groom."

130. Nayf said—not imagining that within mere months a creature of flesh and blood would appear to him—that the lion in the poem was God and that if you pondered, for instance, the unconscious mind or historical determinism, any mystic or metaphysical principle with absolute sway over human life, you would realize that Ginsberg's lion was that thing made flesh and freed of portentous argument and abstraction. He said the lion was the only unreal thing in the poem and yet, for all that, everything else in it was confused and sad and risible; things that made it impossible to go on living. He said that faith, as symbolized by the lion, was what shielded people from ultimate despair.

131. "Remember Radwa Adel?" he whispered to Paulo with rare gravity (perhaps the first time that the activist's name came up since we heard of her suicide four years before): "Basically, she was in need of something like the lion. With everything she did she needed to know there was a lion in her house." And he turned—I don't know why—to address his words to me: "The lion, Gear Knob. The lion or something like it is the only thing that could have protected her from suicide . . ."

132. The evening after I met with Maher Abdel Aziz, on November 21, 2011, I saw for the first time the picture of Alia Al Mahdi, naked, on the Internet. Alia Al Mahdi published a nude picture of herself on her blog. Her contribution to the revolution, as she put it (though the revolutionaries themselves would attack the picture's subject the instant they recognized her during the million-man demo on November 25 in Tahrir Square, their sit-in subsequently broken up, as is the case with all such gatherings, achieving nothing but an increased desire for vengeance between the kids and cops; the strikers would harass Alia Al Mahdi and with blows and insults cast her out, and before anyone could blink the parliamentary elections would be upon us without a single official statement on the dead, not a minute's worth of justice). I saw the picture and compared the defiance of a girl barely older than twenty with that of the Student Movement grande dame who obsessed me. And I thought that somehow Alia Al Mahdi, too, was committing suicide.

133. The evening after I met Maher—and before I witnessed the revolutionaries with their hostility to Alia Al Mahdi, opposing what seemed to me to be both closer to their revolution than any political activism and far removed from the opiates of sectarian war injected through the Islamists' alliances with first the military council and then the U.S. government, far removed from the stomach-turning struggle for a power that would sweep away neither beggary, nor prostitution, nor even the lawlessness of the police—I thought that Alia Al Mahdi succeeded where the activist had failed; and as with her (with Radwa Adel), so with all past and future generations of female activists. Sat before Alia Al Mahdi's picture on the screen like someone

praying to an icon in a church, I thought most especially of Saba and, faced with that ex-lover, felt something between the urge to laugh and retch.

134. There's not one piece of evidence to persuade me that Alia Al Mahdi was anything other than a silly girl, but it was she and she alone—without cause or circle or culture, without political activism or feminist movement—that set the female body naked before us all. She left no space for suspicions that by doing so she in fact sought to seduce or make money. With the pride of someone offering up their soul for freedom in Mohammed Mahmoud Street—something that none of the Student Movement's great and good had ever done—Alia Al Mahdi put her body on the Net. And she said that this was her revolution.

135. I was saying that she called Mojab Harb: Radwa Adel. That she did so after they had separated, as if pleading for help, despite the fact that it was she who'd requested a divorce, on the grounds that Mojab didn't love her. The truth was that Mojab had grown depressed at life in Cairo's circle, after his family had opposed his marriage to an older, divorced communist, and he had traveled south to live with her, putting his job in Alexandria at risk (that's how much Mojab loved her). Because he didn't love her, then, or because she couldn't bear the way her comrades-in-arms looked at her after she'd begun her new life.

136. In the wake of their divorce, in the year before her suicide, Radwa called Mojab; she had just got back from the Meadow Flower Café where she'd met up with former comrades and friends for the first time since the separation and found them

looking at her—she told him—like she was some single woman on the prowl for a man. She was utterly distraught. To accept her wish for a divorce so ungrudgingly after all he'd done for them both: that, I say, is how much Mojab loved her. It never occurred to him to punish her or cut her off. And he did not discount the possibility that her plea for help signaled a readiness to try again.

137. One year before Nayf's twenty-first birthday, while Nayf was discovering Allen Ginsberg and Paulo, Nargis, Radwa called Mojab. I don't know if it was the same call. She told him she was having trouble and needed to see him. The one who'd left him, the one who'd been so sure: she needed to see him. There was something in her voice that told him they were still together, and in the course of a conversation that I reckon must have occurred repeatedly throughout their marriage, Mojab told Radwa that life and work were overwhelming him—he himself has forgotten what he was busy with, except that he was without doubt overwhelmed—and would call her as soon as he had sorted himself out. Two days at most, he said. And he was satisfied that there was something in her voice telling him that they were still together.

138. But when he'd got his work out of the way as quickly as he could and called, that thing was totally absent. In the tones of someone asserting she needed no one, Radwa informed Mojab that she was fine; it was as though she wondered why he'd called. And despite a real desire to hold on to their friendship, as he persisted in calling their relationship, Mojab made up his mind never to call Radwa again.

139. Afterwards, in the summer of 1997, Mojab would hear that Radwa had gone looking for an old comrade who'd embraced political Islam and taken himself off to live in some Delta village: the last place she would fail to find an alternative to suicide. And from the same vantage point from which I view Nargis—and given that Radwa reached this point having lost her comrades-in-arms and Mojab—it occurs to me now that the activist struggled in order to live, and did not live to struggle. It occurs to me that she was just like Nargis, with the difference that she committed suicide for real: that trading on suicide was not enough for her.

140. The night of Radwa Adel's suicide and Nayf's twenty-first birthday, after the announcement of The Crocodiles, we walked to Suleiman Gowhar Street where, past one in the morning, the guests gathered at my family's apartment.

141. My family were away for the summer and we couldn't go to Maadi, where we usually held our parties, to the house of our friend Mizo, plump and white as a dancing girl from the forties. Mizo's mother was an American artist, a first-wave hippie until she embraced Islam in search of spiritual fulfillment, and his father an alcoholic businessman who traveled a lot, so he and his brothers made good use of the spacious house with its garden for their own ends, giving themselves over to "broadening the soul," as Mizo, a disciple of American Sufism, referred to his recreational activities. On any night you'd find three or more groups divided between the same number of ground-floor rooms, in each a different sort of music and a different drug. Freedom of movement between these scenes was guaranteed, as was your ability to sprawl out in some neutral space, naked if

you so wished. And if two, or more, were to go upstairs to one of the top-floor bedrooms and shut the door behind them no one would bat an eye.

142. What went on at Mizo's was, I guess, precisely what the newspapers of the day had begun to agitate against and denounce, claiming that these things were happening at parties on the independent cultural circuit and at writers' gatherings, though with the exception of Nayf and Paulo I never saw a single intellectual nor Nineties writer there. The writers were deeply conservative by comparison, for all that their reputation was mud (as we were in the habit of calling anything we didn't like, in pointed reference to the countryside). Yet even at Mizo's, until campaigns crying heresy and treason and linking individualism to Ayatollah Khomeini's Great and Lesser Satans first started in the pages of *The Week* and *The Constitution*, until the once socially progressive magazine *Roz Al Youssef* performed its volte-face, I don't believe anyone was intentionally setting out to be morally degenerate, exactly, nor held any predetermined attitude towards society's sacred cows.

143. In 2011 I think on Wadih Saadeh, and I remember the suitcase of the future: our suitcase. The suitcase of The Crocodiles Group for Secret Egyptian Poetry, Mojab Harb's suitcase, and ours. We really did not want to carry it. We did not realize that our arrival depended on it. And what happened to Mizo was the first faint sign that there was a future dangling before us, though we had miles to go before it finally arrived. The first sign.

144. So . . . We couldn't celebrate in Maadi because Mizo had been locked up in the Satanism case: the most significant

achievement of the press campaign against dissolution and immorality in the summer of 1997—its victory over treason, collusion and contempt for religion—albeit not one directly connected with the innermost recesses of the circle.

145. Before the case and after, the newspapers' slanders against Nargis and Saba, and those other than Nargis and Saba, never let up, nor did the propagation of rumors—a parallel campaign in which the press were aided by persons, mainly nationalist by persuasion, from within our circle and its fringes—about dubious sources of funding for experimental theater troupes and human rights associations, about plots of cultural colonialism carried out, consciously or unconsciously, by the institutions of the independent art scene, about the moral flexibility of young female poets and their husbands, foreign agents and enemies of the Cause to a man. And no one knew what the Cause was.

146. Our outrage and alarm mounted, though we continued to act as though none of what was written or said concerned us. Only Mizo's imprisonment alerted us to the fact that the space in which we lived was shrinking, that our places were growing too narrow to hold us, to hold our future and what we carried with us to that future; only when we learned that Mizo's mother had gone to pieces and that his brothers were panic-stricken and that we, in consequence, could not go to Maadi.

147. Mizo was hooked on heavy metal and punk and he played in a band. He wore black leather, grew out his dyed-black hair and for gigs would smear mascara round his eyes; sometimes he'd cover his whole face with cosmetics, contriving a mask that left him looking Gothic and grim. Now, I find it difficult to believe

that back then there were no mobile phones, let alone all this multimedia stuff; I barely understand how we kept in touch via landline alone when we would spend the whole time in the street, with no brain in our heads to memorize numbers or jot them down on paper. So it is that I can't remember how we found out about Mizo's arrest; nor do I remember ever seeing him after his release, or going back, even just the once, to his house in Maadi. A mutual friend told me that after his release Mizo gave up the guitar and partying for good, and how true the rumor was that he turned religious, shaving his head, growing out his beard, a prayer-bruise in the center of his forehead, I couldn't say.

148. About a week before The Crocodiles were announced, I was saying—at dawn, at the tail end of just another night that summer—more than one friend lived out the selfsame classic nightmare: troopers from State Security's investigations branch, in plainclothes, hammering at his front door to drag him from his bedroom, brushing off paternal pleas or threats. Most of the fathers were rich or important enough to get away with threatening the officers that accompanied the troopers, but even so, and without warrant, the investigators ransacked these homes with absolute freedom that dawn: they confiscated anything they judged Satanic, then led the young accused off to the interrogation center in Lazoghli, or Doqqi, or wherever it was they were doing it.

149. I think of Mizo because it was his legendary generosity that brought us, about a week after his imprisonment, a vision like a prophecy—the night we celebrated The Crocodiles—and because what happened to him seems to me to have been a milestone on our journey.

150. And so Mizo was locked up and us without a thought in our heads except The Crocodiles, despite the mounting evidence of lions in our lives. Had there really been evidence of lions other than Nayf's exponential infatuation—"Howl," "Kaddish" and all Ginsberg's other work aside—with one short poem entitled "The Lion for Real"? I would later recall a number of related facts: that the nearest town to Paulo's village was Lion's Pool, for instance, or that Nayf lived for a period behind the Giza Zoo where we were all brought up short, at least once, by a roar from one of the lions; that we'd watched *The Lion King* together at its premiere in the Tahrir Cinema near my family's apartment and enjoyed it immensely; and that the headman of the Nineties Generation tribe, old Laith, his name meant "lion" as well. No need to add that Laith is also a synonym for Osama, the name of the man responsible for the greatest terrorist attack in New York's history.

151. While Mizo was in prison and Paulo developed pictures he'd taken in our absence (that is what's important); while Radwa Adel licensed herself to commit suicide by taking another trip, which she knew would lead her to where she'd find no reason to go on living, no alternative to love or struggle (writing or thinking, art, culture); and while Nayf read over and over and over again the poem which consumed him until he had it off by heart, at the same time confirming his skill as a programmer and winning a reputation as a hugely talented technician in this burgeoning field, were we just waiting for the lion to appear?

152. And Paulo said: "The lion's not God. It's not some new alternative to God, I mean, although everything tends to give that impression." It was the winter of 2001, a few months before

the appearance of a flesh-and-blood lion, after two or three weeks spent pondering Nayf's interpretation of Ginsberg's lion. Paulo had just read another rendering of the poem. I don't recall where we three were. All I remember is being aware that Paulo had suddenly grown taller and noticing that since Millennium Eve he had become frighteningly thin. Overnight his face had regained that very inflexibility that had once made it so hard for us to credit the purity in his smiles, and slowly the creases in his cheeks grew sharper; rage frozen on his lips, eyes dry. But I hadn't been aware he'd grown so very thin. I've no idea where this supernatural power of prophecy came from, and nor did he, but he talked on in limpid tones.

153. "The lion is revolution." So spoke Paulo and us not knowing what his words could mean. And yet, for the first time and perhaps the last in a situation such as this, Nayf's reaction contained no trace of contempt for what Paulo said. He did not gaze on him with a mock reverence, nor did he nod his head in a caricature of the humble student heeding his wise master, but really seemed to be listening: "That's why he arrives so hesitantly but takes his leave with fireworks. And that's why, as well, he says that he'll return: revolution always returns because it always leads to repression. The lion is this repression. What's repression? It's the energy that can negate itself. The lion is the charge of freedom that makes men revolt and the lion is the repression latent in that revolution. You spend your life struggling only to discover that your struggle was opportunism and another struggle starts to set this straight. You're familiar with opportunism? The lion is the act of struggling, with shabby opportunism, for the sake of a freedom that might morph at any moment into repression."

154. I recall Mizo, one evening in 1995 or 1996, bursting in on us at the Horriya Café in Bab Al Louq with a volume of selected translations from Jalal Al Din Rumi's *Masnavi* entitled *Feeling the Shoulder of a Lion* and excitedly banging the book down on the small table, panting: "Heard the story in this book, man?" Half laughing, he saw its corner had been wetted in the bowl of *tirmis*, a bean skin or two hanging from its cover. (It makes me laugh now that Mizo, with his English and his alienation from Egyptian culture, was a true believer despite his diabolical appearance: before he was imprisoned in the Satanism case, Mizo would describe himself as a Sufi and repeat ad nauseam that Mohammed was "a totally cool prophet" and no religion on earth was better than Islam.) Downing one bottle of Stella after another, Mizo told us the tale.

155. *A peasant tethered his bull in the stable. A lion came along and ate the bull, then lay down in its place. Late that night the peasant ventured out to check on his bull and groping in the corner his hand passed back and forth across the lion's flank. He felt one shoulder, crossed the breast and felt the other. The lion thought: Were a light to sweep away the veil of darkness that hides me from him, this man would straightway die of what was thus revealed . . .* For Mizo, in his drunken state, this lion was a compelling symbol of the truth of God's existence.

156. And Mojab Harb said that Egyptians, despite their claims of piety, were really atheists. Just a few weeks ago, it was, after his argument with an Egyptian colleague in Kuwait over the photograph of the female protester whom the military police stripped naked, stamping on her breasts. The colleague had blamed the girl for demonstrating, as though that in itself

excused what the soldiers did with her . . . Mojab said that they "worshipped all the pagan idols in the name of a god they neither knew nor wished to know. They picture a god cut to their own opportunistic cloth: duplicitous, hypocritical, petty, superficial, stubbornly ignorant, his noble ends no bar to ignoble means." Mojab was talking of course about the silence of the Muslim Brotherhood and Salafists—not to mention the Couch Potatoes watching silently at home—as the army murdered its people in the streets, but basically he was talking about the lion's absence: He who is blind to the lion in life is blind to life itself.

157. Fifteen years on from Mizo's fable, about a year ago now, I would recall Paulo's interpretation of the lion in Ginsberg's poem as millions streamed out of Cairo's mosques onto the streets after the Friday prayers to rail against the Interior Ministry. And I felt that God had appeared for real. It was January 28, 2011. The morning of Saturday, January 29, before washing away the traces of twenty-four hours of sprinting and stopping and squatting on pavements, of cheating tear gas with fizzy water and vinegar and onion, I sat on the steps in the entrance of the building where I lived in Manyal, then ascended to my apartment.

158. I remember gaping blankly at the sky until my attention was caught by thick smoke rising from somewhere beneath the sun and altering the color of the clouds and it struck me that there was no contradiction between Paulo's interpretation and the original interpretation offered by Nayf: The lion was revolution because the lion was God; when revolution comes—and leaving religion out of it—then God appears. I remember I said something of this sort to myself, then added out loud: "Your blessings, O Lion!"

159. As a result of his battles and resulting injuries the male lion rarely lives longer than ten years in the wild. "Settled," he lives off his pride of lionesses, who feed him in return for his protection and his seed; only the lionesses hunt and raise the cubs of both sexes. Yet though the female remains in the pride after she has grown and learned to hunt, the male is expelled the moment he's a cub no longer and is forced to find food for himself . . . until, that is, he chances on a suitable pride of lionesses and defeats their elderly patriarch to take his place. It might happen that he allies with another lion or two and together they attack a pride and take it for their own. The new incumbent is like a conquering king before his captive foes and even before pawing up the soil and pissing like someone building walls about his dominion—even as the mother resists him with everything she's got—he slaughters his rival's offspring to set the desire coursing through the females' bodies and enabling him to get them pregnant again. Without a pride the lion becomes a wanderer, which is what happens, too, to the old defeated leader after the battle's course is run.

160. It occurs to me now, thinking about Mizo's imprisonment, that the difference between the settled lion and the wanderer is the difference between peasants and Bedouin. It strikes me that we were peasants, dreaming we were Bedouin like the wanderers of the Beat Generation, and that the vagrancy we so cherished could not erase our need for lionesses that we never found within the circle. We were peasants playing at Bedouin, and we never quite believed ourselves. In the light of what would take place in 2011—regardless of the dualities and contradictions, regardless of what we wanted and were able to be—we were the cubs of submissive lionesses, slaughtered by blood-crazed

fathers. Despite the good they were meant to want for us and for our home, and maybe in its name, they slaughtered us.

161. The evening after I met Maher Abdel Aziz, on the eve of the second, abortive mass movement and what was dubbed the Alia Al Mahdi scandal, it would occur to me that the revolution was nothing more than an attempt by the cubs to stop the new incumbent killing them unchallenged. Until a revolution offers the chance of such a challenge there is only flight into exile or joining the intellectuals' circle (the struggle heroes, the big thinkers . . .) and it would strike me that a cub's only weapon when faced with a lion in his prime is its naked body, and that the attempt—whether embarked upon by an intellectual activist or just a silly girl; whether embarked upon by baring the body to the bullets of Central Security's riot troops and the military police or by stripping it naked against all expectation and precedent—it would strike me that the attempt to stand up to the incumbent lions (just like the attempt to flee from them, perhaps) is necessarily a suicide.

162. In 2008, after traveling abroad, Adham Al Yamani would publish "The Final Exit": *They had sentenced me to death, myself and two friends; what they called a mercy killing, such as the one that had already claimed a fourth friend. We didn't fully understand what they meant by these words nor what came afterwards, for they'd let us go free, no guards or jail cells, and sentenced us to a kind of execution that they call merciful, the kind carried out by a cheery middle-aged woman; which is painless, but which is death, anyway. Shortly before the sentence was due to be carried out, I consulted with my mother and friends and made up my mind to flee, to which everyone agreed while the other two stayed behind to await*

the woman. Leaving—after they had handed me all the money they had—I came face to face with the merciful lady next to the house. Neither of us looked at the other. She ignored me and went on and I walked on a little way and began to run, looking over my shoulder, in other lands.

163. After learning of Mizo's imprisonment in June 1997, we would realize that the arrests had begun as news spread of heavy metal parties held in the Baron's Palace on Salah Salim Road—that abandoned, some said haunted, Gothic pile, built by a Belgian industrialist and entrepreneur in 1911—and we would accept the way things were until the public prosecutor released our friends for lack of evidence. (How—for nine months straight until the clashes flared up again—could we have accepted the ways things were? How, after taking to the streets to remove the Minister of the Interior, only to end up throwing the president out of office and attacking, or imagining that we were attacking, the head offices of State Security?) And ignoring for the moment their being locked up with no visiting rights, the detainees would be subjected to merciless interrogations amounting to brainwashing, on the pretext of correcting the moral and doctrinal compasses of some hundred or so strayed Guardians of the Future.

164. And because our fathers kill us . . . Some thirty years after the southern poet Amal Donqol hymned futile defiance with his words "Glory to Satan," young men were hung up by their feet and all Egypt stood with State Security. Not because the people love the government but because they hate the Devil; and the free press, the likes of Adel Hamouda and Mustafa Bakri, convinced them that these people performed rituals in

worship of Satan, arguing from the spread of such practices in America.

165. In fact there is no link between heavy metal and Satanism, not even between Satanism and Satan worship in the literal sense—other than black clothes and razor-edged jewelry and makeup, which are also associated with vampires, punk and emo groups and many other idiocies besides—just the claim that if you played a tape or record backwards you'd hear the Devil himself cursing God, something the new "scholars of the Faith" referred to as they depicted yet another deadly plague foisted on us by the godless West, asserting the impermissibility of listening to heavy metal since all music was forbidden.

166. All this, indeed, and no Moon in our lives. But do the people really not love their government? After a year of participating in, then following the revolution I began to suspect that the Egyptians' ingrained hatred for their supposedly unjust government was no more than an inverted terror that this government might fall—the power that granted them life just as it removed it: utterly—because they did not believe in their right to live. As though God really had created them to worship and nothing more, and was not overly concerned with what they worshipped . . .

167. The night of Nayf's twenty-first birthday we gathered at my family's apartment and played no heavy metal, in either direction. Next day I was still deep in a trip that had started within half an hour of dropping acid that night, after I had bribed Umm Atta, the doorman's wife, not to tell my father about such a quantity of young people turning up at the apartment in a

single night and staying till morning—I paid her well above the going rate for cleaning the place on the evening of June 6—and this is why I felt, as anyone always feels who's not a foreigner in Cairo, that the neighbors, even the passersby, were watching me and objecting to my behavior and that as a consequence, something truly catastrophic might occur at any moment.

168. One-eyed Umm Atta; like a fairy-tale witch: at times I remember her with dazzling clarity. Her face, split by an unwavering craven smile, illuminates the mouth of a darkened tunnel in my mind. When this happens she seems to me the living embodiment of everything that's painful in Egyptian society; or, at least, an embodiment of the essence of things like duplicity and exploitation, whatever it is that makes these things a logic to live by. I do know that it's a logic that can purge any behavior of its moral value, and for a reason I haven't understood to this day, I find myself invoking a rights activist I fell in love with, the one whom Paulo dated before he met Nargis.

169. One-eyed Umm Atta: all of sudden I think of her (a gold tooth in a toothless gob set parallel to an eyelid paralyzed at half-mast as she advances): the brute force of her battering at the apartment door and the violence gumming up her voice as she bullies my mother for clothes and food; then her laugh, a knife-thrust lost in the crowd, muffled by her black robe and about her head a spotted handkerchief; in memory, Umm Atta's a meter high, no more.

170. Umm Atta illuminates the mouth of a darkened tunnel in my mind, invoking a tall rights activist with frizzy hair called Saba. She never stopped—the activist, I mean—complaining

of men's privileges in a male society and stuff about the injustice and uselessness of marriage (and me not yet aware that this abuse and contempt of hers concealed a cowardly special pleading for gays and their ghettos—and her a married woman), and at the same time, no sooner had she gotten to know a man than she'd offer herself to him quite indiscriminately, indeed would frequently try to secure full payment up front. There's a blend of self-abasement and mercilessness in Egyptian society, an ugliness of which Saba was the perfect embodiment, but I see it too in the face of Umm Atta, the doorman's one-eyed wife. And when this happens, the terror of it mixed in with the effects of the acid that afternoon of June 21, 1997, returns.

171. Today it occurs to me that what dampened the terror at the time was that I, after taking tea with Nayf and Paulo at the same café on whose pavement we'd founded The Crocodiles—my memory tells me it was Ceylon; green boxes with a white lion in raised profile extending a hooked tongue and brandishing a sword before its face were stacked on the shelf facing our chairs, above the counter, inside the cramped café—remembered what had transpired between them the day before. I remembered what had transpired between Nayf and Paulo and surrendered to the memory, until I was able to return home alone and shut myself in my room in the dark, staring at the ceiling and summoning up what happened as if projected in 3-D.

172. The prelude to events had to have been June 16, 1997, the date of the first violent confrontation between Paulo and Nargis. He was angry that she had only spent one day with him between two trips and criticized her relationship with her son; in her hearing he repeated something the boy had told her on

the eve of his birthday while she was away traveling—"Couldn't you come for just one night, then go back?"—and she scowled and turned aside, then a short while later hissed with glacial calm: "No one—no one on earth—has the right to interfere in my parenting." And when Paulo said it wasn't parenting that was at issue she started to rave and froth with uncontrollable violence. Her rage, he said, was black and mad.

173. That day Nargis told Paulo many things about being civilized, about upbringing, how she was aware of what she did and thought deeply on things, about the worthlessness of having someone close to her who couldn't understand that. But of everything she said what astonished me was something I don't believe I've thought seriously about until today: "All this because I slept with you. There are dozens like you who have got close to me and still respect me. The mistake I made is that I slept with you." After a while she calmed down and wept: "I know. I know I'm a bad mother." Then back to shouting at him, before presenting him with theories, advanced in that well-attested combination of defiance and diffidence, about mothers' relationships with their sons and their impact on the lives of men in general, criticizing Egyptian mothers for the excessive care they show their children.

174. And I remember that Paulo would write—under the title "The Hypocritical Reader"—exactly one day after this confrontation (and after his pocket had been picked in the course of a fight contrived for the purpose): *Something in the crossroads' angle brings back your face to me—as St. T. S. Eliot quoted from our revered C. Baudelaire: "mon semblable, mon frère." Something brings back a miraculous dance you once unleashed, halfway between*

combat and an embrace. But it distracted me, for sure, from your deft hand as it pulled from my pocket precisely the thing my pocket needs. Now it's as though I see your eyes—the comedian scowls when you meet him off-duty because his trade is taking smiles to wipe the scowls from other faces—and it's as though you're the prey, my look-alike, my brother: as though you're the prey and I'm the slashing hawk.

175. On June 19 we were in the garden of the house in Mary-outiya because Nayf had got hold of a bottle of Absolut, which we'd decided to drink on the balcony as we played three tapes by the Sufi ecstatic, chanter in praise of the Prophet, Yassin Al Tohami, tapes we'd never listened to before. And while we were out there the debate between Nayf and Paulo gathered force till a violent fight broke out, like a boxing match. Before the fight broke out, in roughly the time it took to begin it seems to me, we had disposed of the bottle along with a large packet of weed and a whole pack of Marlboros.

176. Once the third and final tape had played to the end, Paulo and Nayf's argument gathered force and I murmured one of Sheikh Yassin's lines—perhaps the one that ran: "And other than the way of love, I have no way, and were I one day to stray, I'd thereby leave my faith"—and there was no other sound but trucks and braying donkeys and just maybe the odd snatch of birdsong; I don't recall exactly when it was that I decided to stay put and sing. Today, it seems strange to me that I was present at the battle from start to finish and never intervened. I think it was the only time that two of us came to actual blows and maybe it was the surprise that held me back, but equally, maybe I wanted to watch.

177. In the garden before us the sun was setting behind squalid, rubbish-sown fields. I remember a distant wall, over which I spied the peak of Khafra's pyramid like the corner of a sodden matchbox and a cloud that looked lit from within. I stayed cross-legged on the ancient couch from where I could hear and see everything. I realized that both of them were right: Nayf voicing a political truth and Paulo insisting on an aesthetic truth. And though the aesthetic Paulo defended no longer convinced anyone but himself, I felt that I would like to know which of the two truths would triumph. I wanted to know which of the two would triumph in life, not in a boxing match, but I viewed the match as an indicator or a prophecy, and perhaps I preferred to keep it fair.

178. Their debate reached its climax when Nayf interrupted Paulo as he was telling us that Nargis had been forced to delay her talk with Ashraf about getting a divorce because her mother-in-law was in hospital. Halfway through this sentence, Nayf began laughing and with the same fixed half-smile he'd be wearing when he informed me of Radwa Adel's suicide two days later, he echoed Paulo in a singsong voice: "Her mother-in-laaaw!" He laughed and patted Paulo's shoulder and said that she was just another shameless cunt. Then he rose to his feet and started to explain, impassively, that Nargis was only attracted to men who could benefit her career. He said that anyone who wanted her was obliged to mirror back to her the mythical image she had of herself (with which she had reinvented the canvas, or woman, or identity). He said that he, Paulo, had to date fulfilled this very role. "Either that, or you'll have to improve her prospects with cash and contacts," Nayf said with another chuckle: "All someone like you could do is

flutter round her, arms outstretched, while she loses her balance and breaks all the laws of gravity." And this law-breaking, I ask myself out loud as I look back at the battle fourteen years on, does it really lead to flight?

179. "You know, Paulo," Nayf added, genuinely affected, the smile gone from his face and Paulo unable to stop him to get a word in in response: "When Nargis found out she was attracted to you she must have been flabbergasted: 'Oh me oh my! I love him and I don't know what do about it!' As long as you spread these fantasies about her she'll stay with you, don't worry. But she'll never acknowledge you, Paulo. It's impossible for her to admit to the relationship. How can you blame her for not leaving a well-off engineer who lets her get away with all this for some kid at Al Azhar University? She's not with Ashraf in the first place. Why do you want her to leave him? Right now the whore's sparking her brain for something to keep you quiet and keep you with her. I tell you, brother, she's hard to stomach . . . Go ahead and tell us about her mother-in-law's illness, forgetting the fact she didn't even go back to Alexandria the time her son was taken to the hospital and she was getting ready for her exhibition at the Atelier du Caire. That was her son in the hospital: her son, Paulo, not her mother-in-law. Go ahead and tell us about her mother-in-law, forgetting all of that business, but Paulo, Paulo . . ." At which juncture the rage surfaced in his voice for the first time since he'd got up: ". . . Hasn't the time come to admit that Nargis is making excuses?"

180. Paulo had made a fourth attempt to speak during this last sentence and unusually for him, there was no anger in his face. I don't know just when it was after that that he was standing

out in the garden with Nayf balled up between couch and wall. I remember a flurry of punches to Nayf's stomach, which he took standing, shouting, "Excuses!" I remember the blood on his nose, though I don't remember any punch to the face, and I remember that when he slumped down beside me and curled up Paulo wasn't there.

181. In memory, Paulo is rising up from the earth after punching Nayf; is upright, floating along as though with unseen wheels beneath his shoes. Slowly, at a fixed distance above the ground, he advances towards the sodden matchbox and the cloud over his head winks out. Like this, then he, too, is curled up after Nayf has returned a blow—I've no idea at what point Nayf got up from next to me nor how he got to Paulo—and then I see them locked together, a pyramidal formation mutating to a dusty ball. I hear nothing but Nayf: "Excuses."

182. Was it really there, or did it just seem that, glinting over the rubbish heaps, there hung a metallic Peugeot car badge, a lion rampant? The snapshot was crowned by Paulo's meaty hand—it, too, turned to metal—that wrapped about Nayf's neck and held it firm; his head, a lump of stone mirroring the rampant Peugeot lion that glinted still, a miniature, overhead.

183. Paulo was now kneeling over Nayf with Nayf still croaking, "Excuses," and twisting until he turned on his side despite the weight of Paulo atop his legs. The second Paulo slackened his grip Nayf swept him off with a swift elbow to the point of his chin, his Adam's apple stretching, then settling back in place as the impact sent the stone—Paulo's head—flying towards the glinting metal. Suddenly, Nayf was standing and Paulo, a ball.

I was murmuring the same line from the poem Sheikh Yassin had sung as Nayf began kicking Paulo's head, as if laying down a beat for his words, uttered in the provocative tone with which he'd started: "A year, maybe two ..."—crack!—"... She'll run out of excuses, Paulo. Three years ..."—crack!—"... She won't admit to the relationship in public, Paulo. Five years ..."—crack!—"... She'll never divorce, Paulo ..."

184. And when Nayf stopped and bent double, clutching his belly, vomiting, Paulo was surveying him with complete calm, cross-legged in the field, feeling his head where the kicks hit home with one hand, and with the other, his Adam's apple. "I'll make a bet with you, you son of a crazy whore." This was Paulo. "If Nargis hasn't divorced her husband by January 1, 2000, I'll give you a photo of what's between her legs. You know what's between her legs? I've got eleven shots; I've only printed one of them. I'll give you all the negatives plus the one I've printed. January 1, 2000. If she hasn't divorced. And I don't take anything off you if she does."

185. The next time we went with Paulo to the developing lab, on June 23, there was no mention of Nargis or the picture. Only, after a long silence, Nayf will say to me: "Remember the heroine of the Student Movement, Laith and Bahaa's girlfriend?" And during the celebration of the group's announcement, the very next day after the battle, despite the fact that Paulo and Nayf will both have a lot to say about poetry, they will only exchange a few, routine words with one another. For most of those invited that night the declared purpose of the party was Nayf's birthday, his coming of age, which meant he was due to receive the money his father had bequeathed to him from

his uncle, the miserly furniture merchant from Damietta. The Crocodiles were celebrating the founding of their group, as they would do everything else, secretly: underwater or—more precisely—in one of those sordid watering hole orgies, snatching meat out of each other's mouths, heaving their bodies out of the water or rolling, log-like, sunk in mud, to a soundtrack of crunch and gulp.

186. We lived in something that resembled a state only in outward appearance (a revelation that would come to those of us who think or read or observe; those of us who've lived to see 2011 and borne witness); we are treated as representatives of a class or sect or even a small family—"You're whose son?" or, "That lot have no religion!"—and not as citizens; it is expected of us that we'll hold wealth and power dearer than anything we, or others, might possess, including those grand phrases about religion, homeland and identity, even though our religion, too, is no religion, our homeland just a place we wish to flee, and identity a life sentence with hard labor. It was expected of us that we'd render sect meaningless, would destroy class itself, in our desperate pursuit of wealth and power, and yet would never cease parroting those same grand phrases.

187. Is it because we're terrified of lions about to slaughter us that we resolved to beg the blessings of the crocodiles?

188. In the evening I think on Moon as reports reach me of the thugs of Central Security and the military police; I give thanks for the file before me and I feel no guilt. I don't know how to say that I'd begun to be bored by the application of formulaic rites and slogans to a single reduplicated scenario—the same

order of events, the same characters, same lies, same crimes, time after time after time to no purpose—a pointlessly reduplicated scenario: shotguns, rubber bullets, a new consignment of tear gas from America, burning tents, stones, molotovs, snipers on the rooftops, live rounds, thugs, You Sons of Dooooogs, the martyr's mother, the number of demonstrators, blankets and gas masks fashioned from scarves, an attack on the field hospital and doctors subjected to assault, we have not and will not fire a single bullet on the demonstrators ... And just as with news of tragedy in Palestine, decades ago, I became terrified that the violence, lies and brutality would no longer affect me; terrified that the murder of innocents in the street would no longer move me, or that I'd go on supporting their demonstrations despite the fact it meant that they'd be murdered ... and not feel a thing. A biting light flares in my head, blinding and paralyzing me, and I awake to a pain in my stomach. Tonight, shall my burning desire to weep be answered?

189. In the evening I look back on Moon's first night with Nayf and am tickled by an incongruous nostalgia. The complex circumstances of their encounter may, or may not, be recounted later. Example: She was wearing a headscarf when he first saw her, only for it to become clear that she was not, or was not always, a woman who wore the hijab. Example: That her hair was coal-black and smooth the first time she revealed it to him, only for it to become apparent that it had been ironed and dyed and that her hair was in fact coarse and brown. The point is that—after a couple of meetings—the two of them were alone in Nayf's flat on the ground floor of a midsized building near the Umm Kulthoum Tower in a street running parallel to the Nile, in Zamalek, conversing about The Crocodiles' philosophy

and the group's place in Cairo's cultural scene (to wit: Downtown and writing). No booze, no drugs, no music even: just reclining, in the breeze of the air conditioner, on the cushions of the large couch—I remember that the couch was a phosphorescent green and the cushions white—with *kanaka* after *kanaka* of coffee, lighting cigarette after cigarette ... For all of three hours, silence was at bay (from the voice of the crocodile, which resembles purling water, to the merit of dividing poems into lines, the talk never ceased) until, with the nicotine and caffeine peaking in their blood, an argument broke out over whether a married woman had the freedom necessary to create art: Moon said it was difficult but possible and Nayf, with characteristic offhandedness, ridiculed the very question.

190. At the second meeting, where, without warning, she appeared to him without a headscarf, she'd informed him with a loud sour laugh that she was a married woman. "Being a traditional bitch works for me," she said with whimsical derision, and he observed that her laughter lent her features a fleeting, but noticeable, ugliness, as though it drenched her face with acid. "I got married when I was nineteen, you know." Thereafter, Nayf would disavow a jealousy which tainted his growing admiration of the greatest poetess of that generation, a jealousy which, he was unable to decide, was either of her or over her: I get the feeling that he was both beaten and bent on victory. His fixation with the lion had lessened since their first meeting and maybe he knew that he would give her all of his attention.

191. Being pure poetry, Moon was the exact opposition of cliché. Yet she was, at the same time, a cliché. Only now, as I look back over her first night with Nayf, clueless as to how it is

that I know all its details, does it occur to me that this explains everything. Despite what I saw in Moon and could not see even in Saba and Nargis, despite the disappearance that in the end made poetry of her, Moon was a cliché. I've no idea what makes me think of American serial killers as, this evening, I arrive at this truth. Those killers with their serial crimes whose star rose in tandem with the hippies, heirs to the Beat Generation, after the sixties blew up in the States: black power, the sexual revolution, the global peace movement versus the Vietnam War (their foundations laid by the Beat Generation: had they also paved the way for those murderous others?). Serial killers are characterized by high intelligence but their crimes are motiveless; their crimes frequently contain an admixture of unconventional sexual desire, but they are motiveless. I thought about them as I told myself that Nargis is a joke and Saba a slogan while Moon is a cliché and that the cliché, though no closer to the truth than joke or slogan, is oftentimes more beautiful than either.

192. Murder without motive, time after time after time. Historically, similar things have happened outside America and before the 1960s—just as moments of liberation similar in style to the hippie movement and Flower Power (the power of flowers versus the force of arms) must inevitably have occurred—but not to the same formula nor as widespread. Just as the new drugs, discovered and developed alongside sexual freedom and the call for global peace, forged a hitherto untrod path for human contact and the rejection of war, it appears that they also forged a path for a new and individualistic form of systematic murder. I thought of serial killers as I told myself that Nargis is a joke and Saba a slogan while Moon is a cliché and that, by writing poetry, we were in fact trying to reach the truth. At

least, we steered clear of the cliché, the joke and the slogan, in an effort to say something else. And for all that, in more than one sense, Moon was the very limit of what we were able to say. And just as the world carried on after the Beat Generation, producing Beatniks like ourselves in America and abroad, it also continued to give birth to serial killers.

193. Following their argument in the Zamalek flat—this happened in the summer of 2001—Nayf would tell himself that for the duration of that first encounter, Moon never looked him in the eye, and he would subsequently observe that the same thing happened at their next two meetings: she avoided looking him in the eye, even at her most relaxed. The sharp words they exchanged would be followed by an electric silence, even though it might not seem so with the two bodies sprawled at ease. When Moon straightened to tie back her hair, puffed out like a tent around her head, her face would be in reach of his right hand.

194. "You know you're a coward?" she said, for the first time staring into his eyes without confusion or uncertainty. She was still tying the ponytail when she looked at him and he couldn't believe it. "I'm the first to tell you?" Not a flicker; just the first signs of a smile upon her lips. "You really are a son of a dog's religion of a coward." And before he could give expression to his astonishment he found his arm in motion, as if of its own accord. "A coward," she was saying, "because you're not ready to put yourself in someone else's place, even in your imagination. You're scared to put yourself in a woman's place because you're scared to ask yourself whether, in those circumstances, you would marry. This fear isn't that standard human emo-

tion with which we're all more or less familiar: there's a moral presumption, a glib contentment with your own predicament. That's why I'm telling you you're a son of a dog's religion of a coward . . ."

195. And this, as I see it, was precisely Moon's genius. When she came out with abrupt and sudden declarations of this sort it was with a tremendous energy, an intentness that summoned thoughts of the weak standing up to the strong, the revolutionary to his oppressor, and she would make the man before her feel, in consequence, that her words issued from some deep place; that she'd thought hard about it and that it pained her. Her subtlety in inferring views, which her self-containment or indifference would not permit her to air more comprehensively, was what flashed in her eyes as her lips quivered. Meanwhile, the truth was that she said things by way of experiment and only cared deeply about their immediate impact—things that sprang from an absolute lack of containment. Moon would lie, tentatively, without believing herself, and the things she said were clichés, even though our admiration of the speaker might obscure the fact. This was the genius Nayf fell for, despite his shrewdness, because it was—as I see it—a genius of cliché, while Paulo and I, with less brains or greater weakness, hooked the Joke and the Slogan.

196. She was saying, "That's why I'm telling you," when Nayf's palm settled on her cheek. And when the palm slid down to her neck she went on: "You're a son of a dog's religion of a coward. Am I right or what? When you said that it makes no difference . . ."

197. It wasn't a slap precisely, though the arm was raised, the palm stretched rigid and the shoulders a straight line through a circle's center. It was like the threat of a slap, which Moon would have returned immediately had she not lost her balance beneath the weight of the slapper, now standing over her head. As he turned to face her she tottered and swayed, until she came to rest cross-legged on the couch, her long summer dress hitched up to show a brown and slender thigh. At which point she looked him in his eyes again. She herself did not know if something in her gaze was different but it no longer fazed him that she looked.

198. A thigh, brown and slender, but aglow and suffused, and her long thick hair, numberless streaked chestnut strands gathered in a ponytail, and her, looking at him. Did Nayf recall the lion? Did the recollection affect an energy pulsing in his body that was like desire and was not desire? A rosy thigh and thick hair and breath of basil with a pulsing energy and her hair and a brown and slender thigh.

199. Moon did not flinch as the palm encircled her nape, the thumb settling on her windpipe, and it did not seem that she was immediately aware of Nayf's other hand tugging the ponytail down as he returned to his seat beside her, chest out this time; only, with the thumb's pressure and her head tilted back, her voice became strangled till she stopped speaking, then a faint whine was heard followed by panting—her lips clamped tight—as though it did not come from her. And though she did not laugh when he hissed in her ear, "The son of a dog's religion is your mother's father," it came as no surprise to him that she didn't resist. "Your mother's father . . . daughter of a *whore*." He

was bringing his face up to hers so that his forehead settled on her nose, as if to crush it. And she was pressing her lips together ever more violently, her breath was drawing closer while her knees parted little by little, further and further.

200. Recalling a gathering of The Crocodiles which took place weeks before that night I can almost hear Nayf cackling derisively at a scene of a masked man flogging two pale buttocks, all that showed of a woman straitjacketed in steel and black leather, on the Internet. How, then, could his thumb now be about to crush the windpipe of a girl kneeling on phosphorescent plush? Later, Moon will tell him that the marks left by his hands and teeth, if she had seen or heard of them on any other girl just a day before that night, would have filled her with disgust.

201. "And yet"—she will go on, with that sour grin of hers that scattered the beauty from her face—"it seems I like abuse and caveman stuff. With you, baby, I've found what I deserve."

202. In 2001, and up till now perhaps, in our conception of civilization—Nargis and Saba's conception, Moon's conception, of being civilized—the sweetness of sex was incompatible with physical violence. Especially when the violence came from a man and was directed at a woman, we viewed it as nothing more than a brute machismo exercising its unreconstructed masculinity; it never occurred to one of us that it might be probing psychological depths quite unrelated to any worldview blowing in from behind the buffalo. Power, possession and absolute loyalty—unlike "evolution"—were things we distanced ourselves from with all our might. A man beating a woman to arouse himself or her would be raping her, subjugating her

body, something that repelled us to the utmost degree. Yet we needed violence more than anything. Perhaps this need for violence—our need to feel the power of possession and a desire for an absolute loyalty to justify our lives, for the temptation to re-create some person in the world other than ourselves—perhaps this was what set Nayf in motion and loosed an energy in his body that resembled desire, yet was not, or not just.

203. So it was that when she did not part her lips as they made contact with his mouth, which had suddenly grown wet, he did not hesitate to lick them, then bite them harder and harder until he was barely stopping himself from drawing blood. And after her hands came to rest beneath his shoulders on the pretext of pushing him away—she wasn't pushing him but pulling him in, planting her fingers through the back of the T-shirt and into his ribs—Nayf was astonished at himself for the savagery with which he bit Moon, cheek and neck and likewise, after lowering the dress from her shoulders and pulling off her bra, bit her breast.

204. Her breast, in size and shape: a lemon; but the nipple was black and very large, a charcoal knuckle, and when his teeth encircled it at the root as though to nip it off—the nipple, I mean—its owner would open her lips wide for the first time and her basil scent would blend with something between pepper and smoke and she would not make a sound. As though the groan that came from her before signified a resistance now broken in the face of a more profound and authentic pain; precisely as though the pain was (and leaving aside what we'd repeat among ourselves, Paulo, Nayf and I, that a person who'd lost pleasure or despaired of it must cling to pain as the only way to feel alive . . .

As I write, in this moment, about myself, I believe that what keeps me alive, confronted by reports of parliamentary elections ongoing since November, is the pain of those twitching on the asphalt after inhaling gas, of those struck by bullets in their eyes, of those stampeding from the scourge of billy clubs and electric cables . . . The pain, that biting light in whose absence no one perceives a thing); as though the pain were, for Moon, the key to a locked door behind which lay her truth, which she would never confess except in jest or without conviction—all her lies in the mirror—and which, consequently, she could not express in any voice whatever.

205. I see him slapping her seriously this time then, while circling her until he stood behind her as she knelt, twisting her arms behind her with one hand and with the other pulling off her underwear, then lowering his trousers to enter her as though ramming a plank of wood into a wall cavity—all this in a single movement, like lightning—and he found her wet and easy—as I was not to find her, at first—and leaned over her back all overlain with gleaming chestnut hair to breathe in the smoke and pepper and search for a trace of basil, which drew further and further away amidst a throbbing pressure, only to return damply with her panting.

206. Then, as Nayf leaned over Moon's back, he would sink his hands into the curve of her flesh and yank her bunched hair, rake it back, and insert his whole thumb into her anus to lift her sex towards him, would reach out his hand to mash her nipple between two fingers, then fall to smacking her rump again. And with the resolve of a saint tortured by Romans on the shore of the Red Sea, she would hold back from crying out—not a

sound except her faint pants broken, despite herself, by eruptions of a lowing or a braying she fought to quell—until the moment that her small brown body quaked, spasm after spasm, having pulled her arms from his grasp and settled on all fours, writhing in something like a fit, a freshly slaughtered panther, biting the green plush as he loomed upright, then knelt upon the couch's edge, his feet still on the living room floor.

207. The oblivious body. That solicits a violence it did not know it wanted. That is offered up in sacrifice to something other than whatever it is that constitutes life in Egyptian society. Far from ideas of for-shame and thou-shalt-not, but far, too, from sticking to principles, no matter how straightforward and true the principles might be. The body, which I, Gear Knob, knew as boisterous, tyrannical for all its triviality, and in which I got to know The Crocodiles' full stink, in one go; maybe Nayf intuited from her silence beneath this pain the truth of its moans. And forgot the lion. As he withdrew from Moon and left her bundled on the couch, still erect himself, yet to come—as he hurried to his bedroom to fetch two scarves and a fat candle in the shape of an apple—perhaps he forgot that a flesh-and-blood lion had been tormenting him for weeks.

208. And I remember that on the night of The Crocodiles' celebration, a little less than four years before all this took place, we had yet to raise the subject of Mizo or any of our imprisoned acquaintances, but even so some scarce-felt weight hung over the gathering. For my own part, before the acid kicked in, I was thinking about State Security investigations and I believe that we were all thinking about similar things though we mightn't have been brave enough to state it openly. Amid an atmosphere

that coiled round the thresholds of even our front doors we were gazing out at a violent hostility towards our very presence in the world, an absolute refusal to accept that the likes of us might breathe God's air or walk upon His earth. And before the acid kicked in—I remember—I pictured them. I pictured them brutish, then I pictured them courteous, clumsily cutting through the garden to Mizo's iron and frosted glass front door as though it were the last frail barrier to a monstrous and inescapable violation. And then, all hope of a comparatively merciful brutishness was gone.

209. I pictured their boots like rocks clattering across the pink marble square set at the center of the wooden flooring of Mizo's circular hall and their ravening eyes sweeping over the eccentric furnishings: the couch with its wine-red pillows on which I'd sprawl to let my sweat dry after dancing or taking MDMA; an original Kandinsky; a red Rothko; a gigantic phonograph bracketed by two wardrobe-sized speakers—I remember Paulo, on Ecstasy, hugging one and pressing his ear to its surface as if to suck up its deafening electronic beats—and the music player connected to the speakers, hidden behind the phonograph; the slim white-wood-and-rubber shelves bursting with books that you, were you to look on them with an ayatollah's eyes, would find Satanic, each and every one.

210. Before the hit kicked in—I was saying—I pictured the men of State Security and pictured their eyes, as though they'd uncoupled from their owners' faces to float through doorways behind which, sinking back against the dark-hued walls, into the exotic carpets and rugs, I'd lost more than one innocence. Nor were their eyes ravening as I pictured them; they were

damp with equal parts gloating and dazzlement and no sooner dry than possessed by a severity that emptied all the world of joy, a severity like the flip side of fear.

211. Acid—I must make clear—was a rare treat, a gift we'd take when celebrating. In those days chemical stimulants were confined to the medications you could buy from the pharmacy (Parkinol, a medicine for epilepsy whose hallucinatory side effects earned it the street name "Cockroaches" and the poor man's heroin, a cough syrup called Codafen), but Paulo had obtained from Mizo—a few weeks before his imprisonment—a bottle like a pen cap filled with five or six drops of LSD. During the party, out of sight of the guests, I took it to the kitchen and tipped it onto a sheet from my notebook, then cut out the saturated part and divided it into three rectangles, one of which I swallowed on the spot with Nayf and Paulo each taking a rectangle for themselves. The trip was certainly strong enough to etch my surroundings in my memory. I can't be sure, but to this day I remember that on the page I used was written in a large and slanting hand, "Most of them are fools, most are braggarts, and abuse is easier than understanding," and that I smiled to read this phrase wondering as I snipped it just when and why it was set down.

212. It's said Jim Morrison, the poet and lead singer of The Doors, saw his death before he died. Jim Morrison, famous for taking acid and hymning death or "riding the dragon" to the life beyond: only now do I recall the story of how he foresaw his death in Death Valley, in 1965. And for the first time in seventeen years I'm struck by a suspicion that what happened to Paulo, Nayf and me at the end of our celebration of The Croco-

diles Group, the afternoon of the day after the announcement, was an echo of what happened to Jim Morrison in that story.

213. I couldn't say how much the acid had to do with it all, but the night before it happened—the night of the party—was my first experience of having people in your home you didn't want to be there, not because you hated them or because they weren't like you, but because whatever it was that bound you together and set you apart from society at large had become a source of fear. As though you were the infected in a time of plague or Jews under the Nazis, your gathering together in one location transforms it into quarantine, a ghetto. It's not pleasant to see your house a ghetto, but it strikes me now that the whole world was turning into a ghetto and it is that, all else aside, that wasn't pleasant. When the dawn prayer call came—I remember—I stopped up every chink that might let in light to delay the coming of the day. And when I heard the call of the kerosene seller followed by the ragman—those familiar cries, steeped in family mornings and dazed awakenings—I slithered up to Paulo sitting cross-legged on the floor, still rolling cigarettes to the voice of Cheikha Rimitti.

214. "When will the jungle be still that the crocodiles might come out?" So I whispered to Paulo. A moment's hesitation, then he began to cackle—Paulo had a way of breaking into laughter a few seconds after the joke had hit: like he was frighteningly upset with you, but had let it go and took the anger out in laughter—and he tipped his head at Nayf, who was on his feet behind us, capering round one of the remaining guests, a Spanish girl: "When the chimp chills out, perhaps."

215. I remember that no sooner had he said it, Nayf turned into a chimp for real; and we watched him, unable to stop laughing. But the chimp didn't chill and the jungle was not still. Even after everyone had left there was still a sense of bustle and noise and by the time we three were slumped on the floor, each one's back against a different wall in the front room, without music or guests, the feeling persisted that I was in the middle of a rowdy ghetto and my comrades swarms of questing ants. Instead of peace or talk of poetry something quite unexpected happened. A tableau or vision. And today I can't say if it actually took place or whether my memory made it up, not to mention the acid.

216. I never broached the subject of what I saw that morning with either friend although I was certain they both saw it, or saw something equally menacing. Maybe each one of us saw something a little different from the others.

217. It's said Jim Morrison saw his death in the Mojave Desert, home of the Joshua tree whose spiny branches are associated with the hippies (free love with the sky your ceiling and plants venerated by the Mexican tribes; prayers for global peace beneath Flower Power's banner). It is in Death Valley, to be exact, that Jim Morrison's said to have seen his death. That part of the Mojave they call Death Valley.

218. It was right after The Doors had formed, in 1965, and the poet was out in the wilderness in the clutches of a powerful trip. It's said he took successive hits that day, then drifted out of sight of his companions. Something was drawing him to a teepee (unclear if it was actually there). He knew he shouldn't obey this thing and that he shouldn't cross the teepee's threshold in

particular; he knew it belonged to a family of Native Americans he'd seen die in a car accident when he was four years old (the incident had haunted him since 1947) and that some awful truth awaited him within.

219. Jim Morrison knew that an awful truth awaited him on the far side of the teepee's threshold and yet he ducked his head and passed through the opening—the sun's disk at his back—into shaped shadow, and there he was, in the Parisian apartment which he would later live in for real, but not till 1971.

220. 1965. No sooner had he entered the teepee in Death Valley, it's said, than Jim Morrison was in Rue Beautreillis on the Right Bank of the Seine and it was there, in the bathroom of a Parisian apartment he would live in a full six years on from that moment in Death Valley, that the love of his life, Pamela Courson, would find him dead in the bathtub, the hair dryer in the water between his legs.

221. It's said that it wasn't the electricity that killed Jim Morrison but a dose of heroin he'd snorted by mistake, thinking it was cocaine, before giving his body over to the bathtub's water. So now, a full six years before the day he snorted the dose, he ducks his head and steps over the threshold of a teepee he knows to belong to the dead Indians whose ghosts have haunted him since childhood, to find himself on the other side of a future that dangles down abridged, cut off, as is the destiny of all glorious men. From the damp hallway to the living room—the doorway of the main bedroom framing an imposing bed, or so I imagine—he traces the path his sweetheart trod the day she found him dead: along the passage leading to the bathroom.

222. The bathroom door's ajar exactly as it would be in 1971, but Jim Morrison—just as Pamela Courson would do the day she found his corpse—must slide along it and turn his head before he sees. He must slide along the door and turn his head and when he turns his eyes to the back of the bathroom—only then—he sees. He sees his body perfectly still, its slack mouth, its two dead eyes.

223. The front room of the apartment in Suleiman Gowhar was triangular in shape and, though cramped, had mirrors and windows that gave the illusion of endless space, especially if you stood parallel to a wall and looked along its length. The night The Crocodiles was announced I'd pulled back the carpets to reveal the mosaic tiling. In the morning, once everyone was gone and I'd switched off the lights and no light remained save a stubborn glow that found its way through screen and curtains, we three lay stretched out like the stopped hands of a clock. A clock whose circular notched track gradually rose out of the floor, a circle within the triangle, as the room's walls bowed outwards. We lay stretched out in silence, Suleiman Gowhar's din reaching us muffled and swelled, its discordant melodies compacted into a single distant howl. And why we didn't move or make a sound, I couldn't say.

224. All of a sudden I became aware of the floor's center point, where our feet were almost touching, where the tiles formed a narrow circle ringed by six shoes like a leather balloon that something was inflating from beneath, the circle turning into a half sphere sticking from the ground, all but pushing our feet back as the walls bowed outwards and all straight lines vanished utterly, nothing left but a conical mound that we ourselves

formed part of. I swear to you that our bodies were canted off the ground, cocked towards the cone's summit like struts supporting the edifice from within. Defying gravity. Our heads stuck fast to the wall and our bodies canted upwards. And yet, nobody spoke. I couldn't tell you what we were all feeling at this stage in our vision, only that something out of the ordinary was happening and we had no option but to go along with it.

225. One of the effects of LSD is that the person goes along with what he sees or thinks he sees. And maybe that's the reason why we didn't speak or even glance at one another the whole time: the tiles bellying out, their color and texture changing, and all the while the howl, which had started to grow louder and more intense, then us, clock hands turned girders. And we could feel our bodies fusing with this new substance that was seeping out from everywhere, hardening into their canted position, suspended in air, transforming slowly into stone. This then was the substance: stone or some kind of marble. Everything was turning into marble while the howl grew louder and took on a deep and dreadful note as though issuing from a bottomless throat. I remember that when I focused on the sound I felt nauseous and told myself that this could only be a lion's call, a lion roaring dementedly at the stampeding herds. Yet I also remember that it reminded me of a great number of people gathered in a circular arena and screaming, while I stood nearby.

226. As though I was telling myself—or as though someone who resembled me in some far-off place had managed to slip inside my head to tell me—that I was part of a circular marble structure raised up to occupy the space where my body had been, and that this structure was a kind of plinth, in the shape

of a cake. That evening, after I'd thought back to the battle between Paulo and Nayf and while the doorman's wife swept the spot, which had now returned to being a regular, triangular front room, I would visualize the structure that had replaced my family apartment as a marble plinth missing the statue for which it was created; just like that, without warning, the cake which ate us was clear before my eyes.

227. Four more years would pass before I made the connection between what I'd seen and the plinth on which it was decreed during King Farouk's reign that the Khedive Ismail's statue would be erected, and never was. Out of nowhere I would learn that the plinth remained as it was—statueless—until on January 25, 1972, Amal Donqol wrote his poem "The Song of the Stone Cake" during the student protests that moved from Cairo University (where Radwa Adel was arrested) to Tahrir Square. One day in October 2001 I would take out his collection, *The Testament to Come*, to read: *The dread hour tolled / They stood in her lifeless brooding squares / And spun on the plinth's steps / Trees of flame / Wind storming through their tender clustered leaves.* And I would ask myself in a panic: Was the thing we heard four years ago, while we were turning into marble—the vegetable market's clamor like a howl that gathered till it became a roar—was that the chanting of the Student Movement's leaders as they demonstrated in Tahrir Square?

228. As I've said, the vision was not mentioned, not at the time and not in 2001. It was not until March 2011, after the revolution, that I learned that the Tahrir demonstration of 1972 had also taken place on January 25, when I read an article by Mona Anis about one of the Student Movement's most famous fig-

ures, Ahmed Abdullah, who died of heart disease in 2007, mere months, as it happened, after my own mother passed away. Only it would seem to me, in the aftermath of Millennium Eve to be precise, that the hostility we gazed out at from our doorways as we celebrated the founding of The Crocodiles following Mizo's arrest in 1997, lay within ourselves; that our worldview and the limits of our imagination—each time we used society to justify our behavior or silence—were both expressions of that very society (was this why we'd kept quiet between August and December 2011, when the army revealed its true nature and citizens were murdered at their soldiers' hands?), and that the rage and dread we harbored was the natural result of these justifications.

229. Nothing was ever mentioned. And though we went on acting as though what was written in the papers didn't concern us, it seems to me that what we guessed at when we felt that the space in which we lived was shrinking, that our places were growing too narrow to hold us and our future, was that we, with our myths and disappointments, with the stories that made lovers of us before there was ever a chance to sincerely question if we were really poets—with our revolution, even: that peaceful protest which was co-opted after being repressed, repressed repeatedly until it was co-opted—that we were the ones who were shrinking the spaces and narrowing the places. As though we, with our transformation into a statueless marble plinth, were in fact taking possession of the suitcase of the future. And of course there was no way we would recognize it.

230. And though we continued to act normally, it strikes me now that those shrunken spaces where we lived—the places

that narrowed about us in the nineties—were the very places where the security forces corralled us when we took to the streets and which one thousand five hundred martyrs or more and one whole year were not sufficient to make wider.

231. In the evening I think on Moon as reports reach me and I laugh to hear the protests are still peaceful. I congratulate myself for opening The Crocodiles file and I feel no guilt. I feel no urge to run through the streets and inhale gas and with the same defeatist logic that's helped me live in Egypt since 2001—"post-despair" Paulo calls it—I can't see that my presence among the hundred, thousand, million unarmed souls exposed to gunfire, run down, snatched, would either help or hinder. I feel I've run quite far enough in previous months and that all that my death might achieve would not outweigh my sister's grief, though her sadness at my loss might last no longer than a few days. I sense a biting light that leaves a sharp pain in my stomach and I consider, with a gravity quite new to me in this context: All this so the military council steps down? Fine. And when the council has stepped down? A biting light, a swelling certainty that the council's fall cannot bring anything that might outweigh a sister's grief over her brother, though her sadness might last no longer than a few days.

232. I think on Moon and remember that she did not return Nayf's violence during their first night together. Joyfully she told me it had left her unable to breathe: she'd spent ten days—during which they did not meet—as though honoring his hands and cock and tongue where her orifices had taken them. And it seemed to her that on the couch new orifices had opened up to take his tongue and cock and hands. It would be another

week, during which they did not meet, before she saw the point of hurting him. And when, trembling, she dealt him the first slap to the face on their fourth date—her eyes on his waist the while—it made her laugh to see him spring immediately erect: that same sour ugly laugh. He had to devise a fresh torment in response, which at last allowed her to scream as he performed it. And her scream filled him with joy.

233. Their third encounter lasted, as would they all, for two days straight. Nayf would skip work to be with her when she turned up outside his weekly two days off, then patiently bear ten days or more of disappearance without asking where she'd been, having assumed she was with her husband ... until she started talking about her temp jobs, like the one he'd met her at (and which she'd left within a fortnight to start another like it), and hinting that these jobs required her to live alone. For the first time in his life, despite the lion's continuing presence, Nayf burned to know all. He began to see Moon as part of a movement, a school, a craze: the Secret Poet's perfect challenge. And before he knew it, this craze or school or movement had him in its grip. He began to be consumed by the desire to control her time and movements; he began, his questions pressing her harder, to notice her lies. By turn he punished her and pleaded so that she'd tell him where she'd been, would keep in touch, would spend more time with him. But she never gave in. "Your problem's that you forget, baby," she'd say. "I'm a married fucking woman."

234. Their first night together, then—Nayf returned with scarves and the apple candle, which he hurriedly lit on the arm of the couch, muttering, "You know you love hot wax; I could never

deny you something that you love"—she looked at him in genuine disbelief, then fought back—in shock—in vain. She stayed silent as he, determinedly and with a deftness that surprised even him, bound her hands behind her back with the scarf until her arms were quite immobile, then pulled her by the nipple to where the flame rocked gently and gave off a faint apple scent—tenderly kissing her neck as he went and murmuring, "Here you are baby, you'll feel the wax in just a moment"—until he'd dumped her down on her belly and squatted on her back, his feet at her flanks, candle in one hand, lighter in the other. And even when the first drops fell, viscid, heavy, sore upon her skin (Nayf following the scene like a sports commentator, cheering every stinging drop as the red wax straightaway cooled, sinking into the flesh to seem like scabbed blood), she writhed and mumbled, mumbled and did not scream as the drops seared her thighs.

235. I remember that the smell of smoke and pepper faded bit by bit as this went on now mingled with that of the wax and that, even so, there returned to Nayf's nostrils—with all its first intensity—the scent of basil.

236. That night, as Nayf at last came down Moon's throat before freeing her arms and leaving her to bandage her body and shower—up to the last instant his hand was in her cunt, bringing her to climax as first his cock, then tongue had done—he was astonished at his cruelty and dexterity; he felt—as he would later tell me while he complained about her in some other context—that the force which spurred him on when he was with her existed outside him, that its source was greater than him, or anyone else: the same propulsive force that drove

him to translate Allen Ginsberg. And for the first time it struck him that Moon and the poem were the two verges of a road whose length was the lion, and that he was walking down this road towards some climax, a beginning or an end.

237. I said I slept with Moon though I can hardly believe it really happened before the story's end; I can't believe that I stroked her short chocolate-colored hair as her slim electric body rose up between my arms. But our pleasure was not tainted by pain. Maybe I loved her a little; maybe all that moved me in her presence was what there was inside me. Following our transformation from respectable young things gone astray to crocodiles, we went on acting as though the writing on the wall was not for us. That's the point. And with our transformation into a statueless marble plinth in 1997, we took possession of the suitcase of the future.

238. Until what happened in 2001 had actually happened we never doubted for a second that we had ventured out and come home safe. The days went forward one after another, out to the end of a rickety wooden plank, while we rolled along in their wake—as for myself, my father would die in 2004 and my mother two years later—but of all things we were closest to the events of 2011. And before it occurred to us that we might be on one side in a changing world—and with a nausea, with a primal terror of being prey, with a dim sense of belonging to a hateful place—we were chanting, ten years later, in Tahrir Square.

239. When Nayf's translation of "The Lion for Real" was published, ten years after it was made, it would attract the attention of a poet called Mahmoud Atef, who could be thought of as

belonging to the generation after The Crocodiles. Atef had nothing to do with secret poetry, but just as we were slightly younger than the Nineties Generation, so he was slightly younger than the leaders of the next (and most of them didn't write poetry), the likes of Ihab Abdel Hamid, Mohammed Khair and Nael El Toukhy, who translated Hebrew. And like Mojab Harb, Atef was a renegade Muslim Brother. He would notice the poem just as he was embarking on his first serious relationship, and, because between themselves he and his girlfriend called his cock "the lion," he would interpret the poem's lion as a symbol of the male member, as though Ginsberg had been addressing his prick when he wrote: *In this life I have heard your promise I am ready to die I have served / Your starved and ancient Presence O Lord I wait in my room at your / Mercy.* A lion *rigid with lust,* Atef would write, implying—with no knowledge of what we were going through—that the lion was the only thing on which the suitcase of the future could be hung.

240. So it was that the third interpretation of the poem would follow in the wake of the first uprising, before the army was deployed to protect the protesters who occupied Tahrir Square from attacks on a sit-in taking place that, had they not protected it, would only ever have been limited and patchy—a belated revisiting of the first two readings. Nine months later, following the outbreak of the abortive second uprising Atef would have broken up with that girlfriend and would not have forgotten her; and the people's enthusiasm for elections forcibly imposed under military rule after numerous massacres in the streets—in October the heads of Coptic protesters were crushed beneath the armed forces' armored cars; then, beating, thieving, and firing recently imported American gas rounds that caused con-

vulsions and endangered lives, the security forces and army revenged themselves on those calling on the generals to return to their barracks on Mohammed Mahmoud Street by Tahrir—their enthusiasm for elections after all these deaths would seem truly immoral.

241. The thing that made us lovers before we would become unwitting revolutionaries and later turned us into fathers ... Does Mahmoud Atef understand that it's the same thing?

242. Before that, before despair had descended utterly, before sectarianism and idiocy broke surface, this business of the lion obsessed me. And making my way back from Tahrir where I'd met up with Atef the day he informed me, laughing, of his interpretation—it might have been in April 2011; I remember it was immediately before or after the first referendum on the constitutional amendments, when an overwhelming majority voted Yes, playing into the hands of the Supreme Council of the Armed Forces and the Muslim Brotherhood—I thought about Nayf and Paulo.

243. This business of the lion obsessed me. At a remove of ten or more years it seems to me that we worshipped neither God nor the revolution so much as something rigid, not with hollow lust, but with the richest desire there is: the desire, or the temptation, to re-create another human being. More than Paulo I thought about Nayf, telling myself that this remaking, in its impossibility and terribleness, resembled nothing less than the wish to change the world. But poetry was present in our worship to a much greater extent than could ever be in a religion's rituals or a party manifesto. A thing closer to the male member

than to religion or history, a signpost to love or hope; this was what moved us—so I told myself—and were it not for this thing we would never have become poets.

244. That night I walked a long way before returning to my apartment in Manyal (this was before I'd moved to where I am now) and with a nostalgia unlike anything I've known, having come to Galaa Bridge from Qasr Al Nil Bridge and crossed it, I set a course through Fini Square to where I'd once lived in Suleiman Gowhar Street.

245. So it was that on the way to my family home—family-less—I summoned up the atmosphere of 1997: magical mystery microbus tours on Parkinol, between Doqqi and Maryoutiya in particular; boozy visits to the home of Sixties writer Alaa Al Deeb in the same bit of Maadi where Mizo lived, during one of which we heard the poet Ibrahim Dawoud read his poem, "The Days before the War": *We stand before the cafés / As though we're bidding them farewell / And leaving our lovers for no reason... We roar with laughter at silly things / And stop for no reason / And the scene, repeated fifty times over in the days before the war seems / Sad and silent"* (No war in particular, though it might seem so); beside the Al Ghouri Wakala, behind the tumbledown wall that ringed a patch of wasteland, the light of the fire we'd lit playing on the face of Rabeh Qumsan—the most diminutive Nineties writer—as he smoked weed in the darkness; the rattling cough of his fellow traveler Mahdi Al Aidi (who would meet a premature end in 1999), just stepped in from the balcony of an apartment in Faisal where he was sharing a smoke with Rabeh, and Rabeh barely able to see what was next to him— just stepped in to lie back and recite an entire book of verse as

if muttering to himself: *In a room, its windows shuttered by an Alexandrian August / A quarter-weight of hash / And three friends / And peeling whitewash on the ceiling / And stop-start chat...* With a nostalgia unlike anything I've known I summoned up the gentle bubbling flow of the things that had happened and that had never seemed, not once along the way, to concern us.

246. Perhaps that night in April 2011, the night Mahmoud Atef informed me of his interpretation of the poem's lion, was the first time I had asked myself—no answer forthcoming—how I had come to know Paulo and Nayf.

247. And perhaps that was the reason I went to the place I'd once lived for the first time since the winter of 2007, when my sister, who'd stayed in the apartment after marrying to keep my mother company, decamped with her family now that my mother was no longer around (we split the deposit equally). Our building's façade had changed and the dyer's shop was replaced by a grocer's with a doctor's sign fixed overhead. In the entrance a pale youth scratching his knee through a heavy robe who'd never heard of Umm Atta: the fruit seller's boy, become a teen since last I saw him. Didn't recognize me but caught the name and shouted: "They went back to the country two years ago." I had no difficulty reacquainting myself with the place; what frightened me was that I felt nothing. As though the nostalgia had been spent on the way to its source, or had never been for the apartment. And the same thing happened when I went on to the café in Tahrir Street on whose pavement we'd founded The Crocodiles. The café was more or less the same; just that, as Maher Abdel Aziz puts it in one of his finest poems, "Its place had shifted four blocks along." And yet: no nostalgia and

no lingering. The walking had tired me out but I did not stay for a tea; I stopped a taxi first chance I got, thinking about Jack Kerouac.

248. The night Mahmoud Atef informed me about the lion, then, I left Doqqi with my mind on the final paragraph of *On the Road*— "So in America when the sun goes down and I sit on the old broken-down river pier watching the long, long skies over New Jersey and sense all that raw land that rolls in one unbelievable huge bulge over to the West Coast, and all that road going, and all the people dreaming in the immensity of it, and in Iowa I know by now the children must be crying in the land where they let the children cry, and tonight the stars'll be out, and don't you know that God is Pooh Bear? the evening star must be drooping and shedding her sparkler dims on the prairie, which is just before the coming of complete night that blesses the earth, darkens all the rivers, cups the peaks and folds the final shore in, and nobody, nobody knows what's going to happen to anybody besides the forlorn rags of growing old, I think of Dean Moriarty, I even think of Old Dean Moriarty the father we never found, I think of Dean Moriarty"—and it occurred to me that I should search for it online and translate it, then make a "Note" linked to a status update on Facebook, adding the phrase "Long live the 1997 Generation."

249. For all that, 1997 came and went without anything super-natural occurring in our lives: Paulo and Nargis fell in love; Nayf became obsessed with the Beat Generation and Radwa Adel split up with Mojab, and Paulo and Nayf made their bet a day before the celebration, then there was the vision of the stone cake just after Radwa died, on the morning after the party,

and two days later Nayf informed me of her death on the way to the developing laboratory. But everything that happened, so it seemed to me, happened in anticipation of 2001. And we'd become adults, for real, before we realized it had happened.

250. All of a sudden we grew up. Sometime prior to Millennium Eve and after Paulo split up with Nargis: suddenly, just like that. And though I don't recall the precise moment I know that it took place during that week, the last of 1999. I know that it was a single moment and that it happened to all three of us, regardless of whether we were independent yet or had our own sources of income or homes, and regardless of the fact that two of us had tasted love and lost the greater part of their goodwill in the process.

251. And since growing up, if only half-consciously, while I hunted in the circle for some girl with a predisposition even the slightest bit sincere towards love and creativity, just one girl from all those who talked of independence and breaking barriers or even practiced it to some degree, who in exchange for happiness would throw over assets like a wretched family or a CV that had no relevance to any real career, a social standing propped up on male friends and their benefits, or a fame so worthless it was comic, being confined to the circle—since the mid-nineties I've been reviewing the same old faces.

252. We grew up and Mojab Harb was writing as we grew, as though he were writing about us: *The booze took off ten heads: / In exchange, we did not lose our souls. / We entered our homes as strangers, / daydreamed / until we had long beards / and when the moon was centered / and the singer had repaired his strings / we*

descended on the neighbors' washing, / kicked doors, tables, chairs, / our loud moans / covering our backs as we returned, / our depths a slight and splintered stone / we cast towards the sea / bobbing on the waves: / twitchy and laughing; / We are the drowsy bears of poetry, / we sit on our backsides and reel about, / we scratch / and slap each other calling the names aloud / so as not to forget; / We go out into the world with drooping lids and dirty shoes: / Where's our share? / Have pity! / Bring us the lover's shoulder, the meat from his tail, / bring us the balls, / From his eyes basil seed falls, / love and carrots mingle on his tongue; / Have pity! / Bring us his sweetheart so we can fuck her on the spit; / One by one we fall into the fire, / our features lift and clear; / Have pity! / We're from good families too; / We're sons of devils and killers / who were passing through, / any one of them could have lit cigarettes for us, / exchanged words / words / words / we talk and have no words, / we talk and our voices' rasp is like a rusty blade, / like a cloudbank of sleeplessness / compressed in our chests, / we talk and have no lanterns. / Your health, Manuel! / Ten pounds of the cups' dregs! / Ten more for the sake of your cross! / We stuffed our hands in greatcoats / and carried him in the truck, / descending to the cities at dawn with running noses; / For our sake / the blood ran black / and at the noon meeting the party disbanded itself; / The killer was one of us, / a mathematician and failed lover / and mathematicians are coming / from locked rooms / their doors labeled Ledgers of the Resurrection and Circles of Hell, / and all with the same smile / of a mouth that cannot fathom joys / they dream of high-walled prisons / and others open to the blazing sun, / they dream of the iron balls/ that drag their chained shadows / with blows of a cosmic pickax / on the white stone / with the cry of Unbelief / in glorious labor unending, / labor without purpose. / Farewell Manuel! / One thing we have: / our thoughts; / No, we've no thoughts, / we will marry that we might have them / and after-

wards, who knows? / We'll carry the lightest of suitcases / and none at all / like the whistle of a steamship parting from the quay, / like the century's half-turn to say goodbye, / like a mantra for death, / like an anthem . . .

253. All of a sudden we grew up and no sooner had we grown than the lion appeared. Nayf's turn for love came late, perhaps because he was most adroit of all of us when it came to life and perhaps because love, seeing as it didn't come until he'd grown, robbed him of more than his goodwill.

254. But everything that happened, happened in anticipation of 2001. I take 2001 as the benchmark, not because it was the year of breakdowns (global events aside) but because, quite simply, it was the year that saw the stories end. And throughout this year those things that had been happening since 1997 grew out, intertwined and gathered force.

255. It was in the first days of July 2001, for instance, that my last argument with Nayf took place. We didn't fight hand to hand as he had with Paulo four years or more previously, on the day before The Crocodiles were announced, but it brought us to a parting, and our parting was a harbinger of what would happen to him exactly six weeks from that date. I don't say I would have protected Nayf from evil nor even that I was a force for good in his life, but it seems to me, looking at the chain of events that began with his bet with Paulo and led to him holing up in the ground-floor apartment which he rented next to the Umm Kulthoum Tower in 2000, the one he spent an entire year looking for with the help of property agents—and I've no idea why he insisted on that Nile-side

spot in Zalamek—it seems to me that our parting left Nayf more alone as the end drew near.

256. Other than Paulo and myself, Nayf had no one to talk to about the lion. And I believe that the breakdown in his relationship with Paulo, even before Moon's appearance, led him to hold it shut up in his heart, till one night, in the front room of that same apartment, we three got drunk in the company of a female Italian archaeologist who lived above him and her friend, a fair-haired Trotskyite singer from Talkha, who was staying with her until she could find somewhere to live in Cairo and with whom she communicated entirely in sign language: "A French lay," as Paulo said of pale-skins like himself who hailed from Daqhaliya, a reference to Bonaparte's men planting their seed out in those parts. In the near future, and from within our circle, too, this girl—who'd call herself Rihla from this point on—would be acclaimed and the popular songs she sang, like Ilham Al Madfaei, to a jazz backing, heard all over. But not yet.

257. This might have been towards the end of April 2001, some two months after Nayf met Moon. Moon was with family in Port Said, or so she gave Nayf to understand. (Did Moon really have family in Port Said? How is it we never heard of them until that moment?) I remember, because Paulo was poking fun at Nayf for fretting: "She should have called by now ..." he'd mock, and laugh. Throughout all this, Rihla was talking to us about religions—that they were all empty: Buddhism and Hinduism as bad as monotheism: mere hurdles before the Fourth International—but she was doing this with a palpable flirtatiousness, so much so that she might as well have said *zarwa*

for *thawra*, climax for revolution, and nor was her behavior any more convincing.

258. I don't know when it all happened. Despite his customary cool, it wasn't the first time Nayf had pulled a histrionic turn out of thin air. Paulo was dancing with the Italian woman and whispering in her ear, then the pair of them would stare at Nayf and laugh. He seemed in a daze over on the couch, with Rihla settled half-kneeling, half-squatting between his legs and asking him the reason for his fascination with a woman who—"as your friend tells it"—was reactionary and backward enough to have engaged in that "counter-revolutionary bourgeois institution-alism" (she meant marriage): "She's really married?" Nayf did not immediately respond, and focusing on Rihla's face I noticed that it was dripping with lust. A lust neither frankly owned nor uncomplicated, but it was there. And in the days that followed I would interpret what Nayf did in part by reference to the pres-ence of a lust like that on the face of a young attractive blonde between his legs.

259. I had an excellent view from where I lay, the remnants of an opium-spiked joint in my hand—perhaps I shouldn't have let Nayf smoke it with me after all the whisky he'd drunk: Rihla's face tilted up towards his eyes and her skirt rucked up off a thigh like a mango peeled and left to sweeten in the air: you know it's sour but you can't resist. No one realized what was happening at first, Nayf rising and appearing to adjust his clothes, then suddenly his straining cock right in front of her lips, his trou-sers round his ankles, and him, barking with a composure that perplexed me: "Suck! Suck, you daughter of a whore!"

260. That night Nayf took Rihla's virginity. He didn't do her straightaway, of course; she had barely averted her face from his cock when he tugged his trousers up and sat back down, presentable again and on his countenance something like apology.

261. I just don't know . . . I was talking to the Italian professor of archaeology as we split a single glass of whisky five ways and Paulo had left laughing after Nayf threatened to throw him out if he didn't cut the crap. I leaned into her ear to sniff the same perfume that Saba used—Guerlain's *Shalimar*—and my ex-lover's scent came out to me from somewhere unfamiliar mixed in with whisky and a sweat which seemed European, I can't say why. And Nayf was sitting on the couch's edge, humming, Rihla lying between his thighs, his thumb in her mouth.

262. I don't know when it all happened. I remember a small fire breaking out in the kitchen, the result of an attempt to make tea abandoned halfway through. The archaeology professor doused it, then disappeared; perhaps she went up to her apartment after she'd said goodbye. All I remember is her sheepish look and her whispering in broken English: "So sad I'm drunk. But some night maybe, my neighbor friend!" I remember Nayf switching off light after light until there was nothing in the front room but the streetlights coming trembling and pale through the window. I remember Shaaban Abdel Rahim's muffled voice floating out of the bedroom, then I remember Rihla, singing. In a voice like a thick ribbon of water surging clear and muscular to the farthest limits—the opposite of Shaaban's scummy bubbles settling randomly about his feet—she sang, "Since you mean to be gone forever, shouldn't you have said so last time?" and Nayf with his eyes closed. I remember the pair of them

completely naked. And when he settled her on top of him, her legs straddling him, when he gave her a hand to bite to fight the pain while the other at her shoulder held her still, her cries, too, seemed made of that same water.

263. Where was I? Did neither of them notice me? Did Nayf kiss her between her thighs before settling her on top? Did I really see her blood upon his knee? And did he know she was a virgin? For a brief instant, as I took a deep drag from a new joint lying on the floor halfway to the bathroom, I saw him pat her head and kiss her face with a tenderness that seemed maternal. He said nothing as he passed over my body in the dark, but I heard him whimpering. Rihla had started singing again as she dressed, then she was asleep in his bedroom. And later, a fully clothed Nayf was pulling me by the arm, to go for a stroll with him along the Nile just before sunrise. I remember his voice cracking as he said, "I'm lost, Gear Knob. And you, you don't know anything," and then I remember him, the sun a blood-red orange directly over his head, breaking down. It was the first time I'd seen Nayf lose his self-control since the night I learned he'd lost his family in a car accident, and he was coming apart with the crying and repeating, "You don't know anything."

264. So, Nayf broke down after taking Rihla's virginity and when he broke he told me about the lion.

265. In the second week of January 2001—so Nayf would tell me in the days that followed, just me and him, relating the details of the story over a series of sessions in that same front room and larding his account with complaints over Moon's absence and her lightweight intellect—while he still wrestled

with Ginsberg's poem, a fully grown lion began visiting him in the apartment where he'd moved two months earlier. At first, Nayf assumed they were hallucinations brought on by thinking about the poem and excessive and continual drug taking. But the lion continued to show up, silent, in various locations about his apartment, once or twice a week, with his svelte body and tufted ears, each one a dunce cap or woolen bonnet.

266. The lion would stay half an hour at most, time spent sleeping or staring out of mournful eyes, Nayf frozen before him, until he evaporated into the thin air from whence he'd come. The first few times Nayf doubted the actual physical existence of this terrifying creature, whose muzzle captivated him as might a child or pet: a cloth flap above a beard as smooth and white as milk. He reassured himself that the lion was just a three-dimensional projection, a hologram, particularly as he never heard it make a sound, nor smelled it, nor found any trace of its presence where he'd watched it pad across the apartment's floor and brush the furniture and walls.

267. But the day he summoned up the courage to reach out to the pale mane, Nayf felt the heft of thick deep fur between his fingers and heard the seductive purr that brought to mind the cat he'd raised from a kitten in Maryoutiya, the times it would perch on his lap demanding love. Before he noticed the jerk of the tail, like a snake with a blind woolen head, the lion had lifted its great head and begun to fade, its features running together until it vanished. Nayf thought he heard the muffled echo of a roar and the lion's jaws yawned to show four fangs like nicotine-yellowed fingers; but the sound was very faint and no one else would have noticed.

268. And from that day on Nayf knew that something in his life had changed. That's what I remember, his voice shaking as he told me that he was approaching some climax, a beginning or an end; teetering on the brink of some ultimate unexampled madness. For the space of a month, the lion's visits continued and Nayf in two minds, considering cutting out the drugs and steeling himself for a disappearance with no return. The poet was weighed down with the terror of his five-and-twenty years as though his professional success, which had made it possible for him to live in Zamalek and drive his own car, to found a literary group and decide to translate a poem, had achieved nothing but a total loss of balance. A loss that left him feeling that he was encompassed by the void and no spaceship at hand.

269. For a year and a half before the lion appeared, Nayf would congratulate himself on his precocious achievements in the face of all obstacles thrown up by life in Cairo. And joyfully, as he regulated the rhythm of his consciousness by tinkering with the brain's chemicals, he'd assumed that he had reached the place where, through his own genius, what he dreamed for himself intersected with what his family dreamed to see him do before they died, and that this was the logical consequence of successfully negotiating his way through those years. Now, he felt that all this success had merely brought him to the moment when his hand sank into the fur of an animal whose very existence was unthinkable.

270. Days before our argument, in casual conversation with a friend of Ashraf's—I don't remember who—I'd learned that Nargis had moved to Philadelphia after her husband had accepted an unexpected offer to lead a research team at the University of Pennsylvania: something to do with combating earth

tremors and water storage tanks. (We'd find out later that she had given to birth to a girl within a month of arriving—which means she had conceived with Ashraf in late 2000—and was nevertheless living by herself in San Francisco on the opposite side of the New World.) The person who told me just said she'd gone and might not return. "She's emigrated, you mean?" Perhaps, he said. And after I'd confirmed this information in a roundabout manner from Paulo, who kept up with her news though he might deny it—"She took off to America, the crazy bitch!"—I found myself alone with Nayf on the pavement outside the Orouba Café on 26 July Street while he, for the hundredth or thousandth time, moaned about Moon.

271. There's a space that grows or shrinks for detailing Nayf's problems with Moon. What matters is that I, that summer evening in 2001 on the pavement outside the Orouba Café, wanted to change the subject and it occurred to me to tell him what I'd heard about Nargis, by way of gossip, forgetting that since Moon's appearance in our lives, Paulo had been doing the very same thing, but to take revenge. He'd listen to Nayf's complaints, then deliberately compare Moon with Nargis, and he'd do so with a bloodless sarcasm, intent on causing him as much hurt as he could (Paulo's chuckles couldn't be called an insect's whine exactly, but every one stung Nayf): "The stoic master of his feelings, the one who saw through Nargis from the moment she got with me ... How come he hasn't seen through the dirtier version of Nargis? Could it be, I wonder, because he's not so stoic when he's with Moon?" And so it seemed like I was talking about Moon while I was actually trying to change the subject: all because the two personalities were frighteningly alike and Nayf did not want to face the fact.

272. And so, no sooner had I mentioned Nargis than he cried, "Give me a break!" "What's with you, Nayf?" I said, and he turned his face away, with singular tetchiness.

273. "What's with you, Nayf," he whispered, as though in disbelief, then he spat on the ground and looked me in the eye: "You're sons of whores," he hissed; I remember the drops of sweat hopping heavenwards off his cheeks. "From the moment Moon started working on the north coast you've been winking at each other: Nargis did this, Nargis said that; 'Listen, Moon's a carbon copy of Nargis.' In the end it's just one guy with a complex about liberated women and one whoreson moron."

274. In my shock I was wondering why the drops of sweat weren't falling to the ground, why they seemed more like a little fountain or spray can, flying upwards in great profusion as his voice grew louder. "I'm a moron, Nayf?" I asked, and he shouted, "You're a faggot. Everyone's done Saba and she's loving it and then you, soon as she looks at you, you start melting, water leaking out of your head. A faggot, no? Paulo's messed up but at least he lives his life and knows what he's about. You, on the other hand, are exactly like a gear knob: you can't shift without the whore you're with giving you directions so you know how fast to move. Ehm eh moooron Naaayf?"

275. The shock had turned to violent anger and I sprang up, setting myself to punch him. But something stopped me. It wasn't sympathy, no. Perhaps I intuited what would happen to him and didn't want to be the cause of harm to his person, but this in itself wouldn't have stopped me punching him. Something like schadenfreude, that's what did it. From a safe remove, I

was looking down on his killing loneliness and gloating. I knew I wouldn't be his friend from that point on, however much he apologized for his words, and I knew that he'd lost Paulo too; he seemed alone and crushed in his loneliness. This was sufficient grist to my mill and I did not punch him.

276. "Fuck you." My interjection as he went on: "You're all failures anyway; your problem is that you're sons of whores and failures." And I left—"Fuck you, Nayf."

277. That night I thought long and hard about Moon's job on the north coast. In the weeks before, when love had got its claws into Nayf and had begun to take his mind off the lion, he was yet to broach the idea of them living together; but he had started to suspect that there was something sexual going on between her and one of the contractors she worked with, especially when she cut her hair short and dyed it an unaccustomed brown, making herself look like some effeminate youth as she stood before him framed in the doorway, whispering: "How d'you like my chocolate hair?" She'd signed up—so she explained—with one of the companies contracted to build resort villages between Alexandria and Matrouh and was staying in a chalet, temporary accommodation she was ferried to and from by company car. The lion had not stopped appearing, but Nayf's indifference to it, amidst his obsession with Moon, had reached the stage where Nayf would go out leaving it behind and return to find it vanished. And Moon did not let a day go past without reporting, or fabricating, details of her stay in the chalet where the contractor spent his nights with her. When jealousy surfaced in Nayf's voice she'd remind him she was married—with an occasional blow to the face or kick to the belly, she'd remind

him—and would rejoice when he expressed himself in kind, at the severity of the torture he'd visit on her body.

278. That night I thought about Moon's new job and guessed—for the first time—that she truly did not wish Nayf well. She acted as though this business with the contractor was no concern of his—since she was married—though she knew full well that loving her put all else out of his mind, even the lion. I guessed that she was doing everything in her power to erase his very person, not to mention his various outside interests and his personal crisis, solely to establish that he loved her the way she should be loved. And I got the feeling that he could well kill her one night and that up until the very last moment even that might not harm her. Always some work colleague and always the justification of her marriage. Was she really married? Moon was playing dumb, in short. And even if she really was just stupid she still reaped the benefit of her stupidity. Moon played dumb and Nayf convinced himself that she benefited by chance. She had no intention of giving him what he wanted, or of settling down with him. And that was enough to crush him, after he'd imagined that their relationship offered a way out of the void that had surrounded him ever since the lion had first appeared.

279. Nayf, who'd had the means to buy a red Mazda at a precociously tender age, then rent out his family's apartment fully furnished, had, after receiving his inheritance in full, kept moving between increasingly chic apartments. (His inheritance: he'd laugh bitterly when he recalled that the amount his uncle had transferred to his account—after telling him, "You're no nephew of mine and I don't know you"—had been no more

than twenty thousand pounds, the price of the car and the bribe to license it.) He had graduated on time from the Faculty of Engineering, Department of Electronics and Electrical Communications in 1998—unlike Paulo, who'd overstayed his course at Al Azhar's Faculty of Education by the time he graduated in the same year—and he did not come to live in Zamalek until December 2000.

280. 2001: the year Nargis moved abroad and Moon appeared, a few weeks before Nayf finished the translation of his favorite poem, in spring. Herewith the first sentence in the account of What Became of Nayf, Founder of The Crocodiles: Moon was never a member of The Crocodiles but she claimed she sympathized with its ideas. In the summer of 2001 she was twenty-seven and Nayf twenty-five, and their first encounter—when he saw her in her headscarf, only for her coal-black hair to later take him by surprise—took place beneath the head of the lion.

281. Since he would frequently sleep over at Nayf's, Shylock—our musician friend who would meet Rihla through me and would contract a counter-revolutionary institutionalized relationship with her in 2003—was the second, and the only other, person to see the creature. Later, when asked, Shylock would deny this, his contribution to establishing the theory that Nayf was schizophrenic, but in those days his relationship with Nayf was excellent and he frequently stayed over. This one time, the lion appeared when they were together in the apartment. And once they were thoroughly terrified, Shylock said he knew a sheikh, a medium with one doctorate in nuclear physics from MIT and another in semiology from the Sorbonne, plus the

highest international qualifications in the field of supernatural phenomena.

282. "Don't stress!" I picture Shylock shouting in his exaggeratedly savvy, street-smart tones, assuring Nayf that the sheikh was equally at home with malign spirits and zoology: "Rest easy, Nouf. A couple of days and I'll set you up with Sheikh Gharnouq …"—"Ghar … what?"—"… Nooouq. No one knows his real name or where he lives …"—and Shylock started whispering, before giving Nayf a wink and going on as before—"Because a guy like that, you know, is going to be watched."

283. *Confused and dazed*—Nayf would continue his translation of the poem, no longer concerned with the way he translated it, despite the multiplicity of renderings, their back-and-forth— *raised up above all things, I remembered there was a real lion starving in his stinking reek in Harlem. No sooner had I opened the door than the bomb blast of his anger erupted in my face. He roared with hunger, staring at the plaster walls, but no one heard him through the window. My eye caught the edge of the neighboring apartment block, red and solid, standing in a deafening stillness. We looked at one another for a long while, his yellow, implacable eye ringed by a halo of red fur. It grew rheumy but he stopped roaring and bared a fang in greeting. I withdrew to cook broccoli for supper on a gas stove made from iron, boiled water for a hot bath in the tub under the sink board. He didn't eat me, though it hurt to see him starve to death in my presence. Within a week, the wasting turned him to a sick rug full of bones. His hair fell out like wheat and rage reddened his eye as he lay aching, hairy head in his paws, before the makeshift desk of egg crates filled with slim volumes of Plato and*

Buddha. I sat up by his side every night, my gaze averted from the hunger of his moth-eaten face, and swore off food. He grew weaker and roared at night as the nightmares chased me down . . .

284. Now, as Ginsberg's own words ring in my ears—read by the poet himself to a jazz backing—I struggle to remember how it was that Paulo, Nayf and I had gotten to know each another. We'd never been regulars at any of the weekly gatherings, though we'd go, different though the two scenes were, to Effat Yassin's apartment in Al Haram and the rooftop in Boulaq Aboulella that was home to the graphic designer Yassin Al Mahdi where Ibrahim Dawoud and Taha Farid Abou Shouma were in constant attendance (they called it the Hermitage) and often joined by the novelist Mamdouh Al Ganaini and Shohdi Surour, son of Naguib Surour, with his Russian features and a rebelliousness that called to mind the Flower Power Sixties. We knew Bahaa Zayd and Laith Al Hayawan of course, but we knew Al Hayawan, who'd die of kidney failure in 2007, better. We knew Al Hayawan better because he, while Bahaa stayed put in Alexandria, had moved to the Cairo neighborhood of Faisal around the time Mojab and Radwa Adel were married. And stayed there.

285. I'm no longer sure just when it was we first met all these people. Now every memory must belong somewhere on the timeline in my head, but I'm no longer sure of where that somewhere is nor of the timeline itself. Remembering something, it's hard to know if it took place before or after The Crocodiles were announced. But the correct answer most likely doesn't matter. What matters is that it happened or that it somehow or other intruded on my perception of everything else: the lavish

suppers hosted by Mousa Al Maghribi (another denizen of Al Haram) in honor of his daughter Hana, by far the youngest of the Nineties Generation's female poets; or our accompanying Laith and Adham Al Yamani, having first met up with them in Faisal, either to those suppers or to Effat Yassin's apartment—it's like I can see them on that street corner now, Laurel and Hardy: Al Hayawan with his mistrustful gaze, short and squat and brown, and the lighter-skinned Al Yamani, tall and broad-chested, yet also very slim, with the sinuous grace of a back-street balladeer treading the boards of some small stage, never ending a sentence in his singsong voice without adding ". . . my friend"—and when we had entered the house to which we'd gone with them, no one would pay us the slightest mind.

286. What astonishes me after all this time is that people kept open homes begrudgingly, and it strikes me that this contradiction between the presence of people in your home and your unwillingness to see them there is the key to this whole period. With a few exceptions, people were stingy with their cigarettes, their booze and drugs, and the women with their bodies—women were scarce within the circle, as they were in Cairene life in general—and though there was a tangible sense that nothing was happening and nobody was getting anywhere given the way things were, we bristled with energy.

287. Why then did we go on playing the part of witness or observer, more so than any other part? At the parties attended by foreign girls studying Arabic, or older actresses and thrill-seekers, or chicks with Arab origins searching for their roots, we danced far more than we talked. When poetry, or what its authors called poetry, was recited we'd hide our faces in

the pot smoke, our stony expressions approximating mockery but never voicing it outright; not necessarily because it didn't impress us—I doubt we listened to a thing—but because that mask spared us dealing with those around us and made us seem implacable.

288. Class distinctions—for me at least—were the last thing we'd admit to among ourselves, even to ourselves, yet it's my belief that from the outset they were the biggest factor in our banding together within the circle. When we first met, Nayf was a penniless engineering student, an orphan living alone in a vast and crumbling apartment that no one had ever cleaned, and Paulo was an Azharite far from home (home: a village in Menoufiya), jobless and of no fixed abode. As for myself, I was studying philosophy at the Faculty of Arts in Cairo University and my father, a destitute doctor, was furious with me. Yet each of us had cause to claim membership of the well-off educated classes—even Paulo's people were major landowners in his home district of Lion's Pool—and deep down we all saw ourselves as respectable. Maybe that's what gave us the bare minimum of self-confidence which allowed us to pursue our ideas on poetry to their logical conclusion; maybe that's what enabled us, each in his way—myself, through detached observation, Paulo, primed for action and accomplishment, and Nayf via his dark quest for life's meaning—maybe that enabled us to voice views we truly believed in, to be impressed with no more than what impressed us or to reject whatever we found repellent in life.

289. In the mid-nineties we were around twenty years old, but we had older friends, and age was never a factor in affiliations

and interactions whose fluctuations and deceptions I'd need seventeen years to unpick. Did our distinctive backgrounds have an effect on The Crocodiles' philosophy?

290. In 1945 the Turkish poet Orhan Velli (whom we read in translation; him, Chilean anti-poet Nicanor Parra and others whose works were translated by Al-Jentil and Bashir Al Sebaei from French and Spanish) wrote that what set poetry apart was its strangeness, its difference from all other forms of speech, and that it was this strangeness that lent it the beauty that made us call it poetry. Poetry's strangeness—Velli wrote—resided in the rules governing meter and rhyme, which began as tools for aiding memorization before it was established that they possessed a beauty of their own. Then they, too, became institutionalized, imitated until their strangeness was destroyed, and it became possible to have both meter and rhyme with no strangeness at all, though remnants of their beauty lingered on . . . What, then, could restore to poetry its strangeness?

291. It must have been in 1994—with the launch of the *Grasshoppers* magazine, edited by Seventies renegade turned Nineties theorist Effat Yassin with the assistance of the young poet Saeb Monzar, and in which Effat attacked nationalism, Marxism and traditional poetic forms until it shut down three issues in, the last of them produced by Saeb Monzar on his own, since Effat Yassin had emigrated to America—that each of us began wondering what he was able to accept as poetry. Between 1995 and 1996 our friendship grew stronger and we started to debate the matter seriously. What could we accept as poetry, setting aside everything that was being written around us and without directly drawing on what had come before? And the first thing

we agreed on was that poetry was located in a place quite distinct and distant not only from the struggle, and the culture and writing against which the various Seventies groups waged war, but also from ambitions of international contacts and achievement—however large or small in scope—and the success they promised; "Beneath the scalp" was the first of our slogans.

292. Poetry (one of Nayf's poems, written during his relationship with Moon): *One day one of them uttered a precise description / of what we know soon as we see it / through the jangle of our words, knotted like pearls / in tight loops about our necks, / as we padded circles round the same old pens, / we paid him no attention; / A crazed dog howled beneath the bridge / and a tow-truck tore at cars / and before it occurred to us to ask him more / the speaker suddenly dropped the description / from the foundation's window; / Another girl or woman started prattling, / reinventing the wheel on a café's pavement, / its cast iron tables ringing to the men's backgammon pieces.*

293. When Nayf went at the appointed hour to the apartment whose address Shylock had given him, not far from Abdeen Palace in Gomhouriya Street, in a building the majority of whose apartments seemed to him to be housing brothels or commercial enterprises of a criminal nature—as I was going to say before the business of when we met occurred to me—the door was opened by a dark-skinned girl in hijab who offered him a formal welcome and, after sitting him down in the bleak front room, volunteered the fact that she was the sheikh's secretary and that the sheikh was not in yet, but he could wait. Then she vanished for a while into a room off a corridor.

294. It would be a cliché to say she wasn't beautiful by conventional standards or that she attracted Nayf immediately all the same. It never occurred to him to approach her, not only because of the headscarf and her trademark phrase "God set it in the balance of your blessings" (which in a single week would become "son of a dog's religion" as simply as thick, soft, coal-black hair would appear where the white cloth now lay like some divine pledge of purity), but also because her innocent, wholesome smile, examined closely, had a sour edge that brought back his terror of the lion. Her presence in this place filled his heart with a fear that he was victim of a conspiracy, a conspiracy that included—in addition to her—Shylock, the lion and that mythical sheikh no trace of whom he'd found. He longed for coffee but she didn't offer him anything to drink; she just sat there as he flipped through a diary and in her eyes a gleam that reminded him of the lion's eyes. And just like the lion, discounting a deep desire whose object he couldn't make out, she stirred something in him, something like a dread of death or of the end of the world.

295. It would be a cliché to say that when you die the world ends as far you're concerned . . .

296. When Nayf went to Sheikh Gharnouq's apartment and spoke to him for what turned out to be a few minutes—a dapper middle-aged man whose build and high-pitched voice reminded Nayf of the TV preacher Amr Khaled, and who gave no evidence, despite the assured air with which he heard out the story of the lion, murmuring a word or two before suddenly quitting the apartment, of having understood a thing, or of knowing anything; the essential difference between the

sheikh and Amr Khaled, aside from the sheikh being older, was the anxiety permanently and plainly displayed on the sheikh's face and his darting eyes, which served to intensify Nayf's fear of a conspiracy and convince him that the sheikh would be no help, in equal measure—the dark-skinned girl in hijab stopped him on the way out and said: "God willing, the sheikh's helped you. God set your comfort in the balance of his blessings." Then she sighed: "I feel like I've seen you somewhere before . . ." And when she finally invited him for tea in the room behind whose door she'd vanished when he arrived, he sat at her desk in a panic, studying the gleam in her eyes until his name came back to her and she cried, "Of course, The Crocodiles! Your stuff works for me, by the way. You'll have come across a poem called 'Blood,' no? I'm the one that wrote it."

297. It would be a cliché to say that for two days following his trip to Sheikh Gharnouq, days in which neither Shylock nor the lion showed up, Nayf hesitated before calling her up to suggest they meet, that he hesitated even more before proposing they meet at Restaurant Estoril in Downtown, and that he was taken aback when she jumped at the idea . . . until, that is, he was ambushed by her hair.

298. From my hypothetical vantage point—as reports reach me so frustrating and painful that I find it impossible to sympathize with even the possibility of revolution—I picture what passed between them as they got drunk at Estoril and am tickled by an incongruous nostalgia: Nayf voicing his irritation at Sheikh Gharnouq and her defending him, only to go on to say she's thinking of leaving the job; Nayf telling her about The Crocodiles and her stating it's the only group producing original

literature now that everyone's ripping off translated poetry or mimicking the few talented voices around . . . She mentioned a number of female poets, appending "daughter of dog's religion" to each name, in pointed reference to the fact that they'd copied her work. She said, "God set it in the balance of my blessings," and cackled, and Nayf couldn't tell if this cackling was to mock the phrase. Religion wasn't raised though she hinted that she'd veiled for the sake of the job, then hinted she was a believer. And when she leaned in to whisper in Nayf's ear, "It works for me to drink with a handsome son of dog's religion like yourself," and he'd caught a distant trace of basil in the air, he observed that this hackneyed compliment left her mouth with a lissome grace which lent it a rare plausibility.

299. And so she went with Nayf to the red Mazda and he drove her all over Cairo—to the sound of Cheb Khaled—so they might finish their conversation; he never suggested she come home with him and she never mentioned her husband— instead, just before dawn, he left her outside her building in Mohandiseen. And he told her, in the course of this excursion, that he loved pain, that pain was the one thing that moved him from within—he didn't mean physical pain, but perhaps that's what Moon took him to mean, from what he said—stressing how she had stunned him with her capacity for transformation. He praised her for maintaining her distance from Cairo's intellectual circles and she gossiped with him. What he said about pain gave her no pause, or didn't seem to, but as she got out of the car, after she'd hugged him, she said, at the very last moment, "Hurting you would work for me. I'll bet your pain is sweet," then whirled round and scampered into the building's entrance before he could reply.

300. Given the whole atmosphere of the nineties, its degeneracy so exaggeratedly depicted in the press—this is what I was saying—Paulo, Nayf and I must have met up by chance. As was the norm in the circle, in all its various iterations, where nobody had necessarily read anybody else yet everybody acted as if they knew everybody, unless there was some handy pretext for passing judgment or some celebrated figure was execrating an unknown—execration, like dining at Mousa Al Maghrebi's, being free—we just assumed that we were friends. But some force field encircled us three, or else we built it around ourselves exclusively and spontaneously, which made our assumption of friendship an excuse at a level much deeper and somehow closer to the truth of what we were, though this truth was then still taking shape and certainly changed. Without discussion or even any thought, we understood that what we projected to those about us was a mask and that we were unique, before we'd reached the age of twenty, in our ability to put on masks. Our true achievement, though we didn't see it at the time, was that not once did we confuse the masks we wore with our true faces. Clear ground lay between us and between the ambition that drove our peers—ambition, if not for fame and riches, then for some idea of an ideal or worthwhile life—and piece by piece it dawned on us that our ambition, though real and powerful, bore no relation to what we saw; that unlike most of those about us we weren't there to become something controversial, for the purpose of impressing or thrilling them, nor were we there to make anything of that nature.

301. For three straight months sometime between 1993 and 1994, as though destined to do so, I kept bumping into Nayf or Paulo or both of them together; and each encounter would end

with us cloistered together, exchanging a few words between ourselves and looking on. With time we began to add a commentary of winks and nods on those around us—this was a significant threshold in our relationship—until it happened that any two of us would ask after the third if he weren't there, and we realized that our enjoyment of avant-garde literary gatherings was contingent on the intimacy we felt when we were together.

302. *One night we left the house of a madwoman*: the opening line of Maher Abdel Aziz's slim poetry collection, published in 2009. It must have been at the start of 1994. We were utterly wasted but Nayf had the devil in him, had energy to burn. Nayf's the only person I've ever known to be made more energetic by weed. And there was this girl with us: nine or ten years old. She must have been the daughter of someone back at the house.

303. None of us had a car, so we walked to the main road to wait for transportation: myself in front and the girl behind me, flanked by Nayf and Paulo on one side and two more on the other. A five-sided figure imprinted on my brain to this day. Nayf, with his Greek physique, handsome as a young Omar Sharif, leaning across the shorter Paulo as though to hug him, so he could reach out to ruffle the girl's hair; fair, broad-shouldered Paulo, his slight hump and big nose, looking back and forth between them and sniggering; then the girl, arms crossed tight against her chest, a half-step ahead of them, her back held straight and step assured while the two remaining friends—featureless—lurch forward on her other side.

304. I can't recall if the girl had been left behind by accident or if she'd slipped outside on purpose, nor why she'd ended up with us in the first place; I think one of us had to deliver her to her big sister somewhere the next morning. Soon as we'd halted on the pavement Nayf stepped up the teasing. She wore a summer dress in the bitter chill and showed no sign of being cold, while we were shivering, and her hair was gathered in a single, thick plait turned by the rain into a length of black dough or a giant worm glistening on her shoulder.

305. When Nayf asked her name she sighed. "May . . ." and her eyes widened into his with an astonishing fixity as she added, "Anything else?" She wasn't a beautiful child but her eyes were so large you saw nothing else in her face, which lent looking at her beneath the lampposts' yellow light a soporific effect, like hypnosis. And when the rain came down, though she'd not lost her composure for an instant while Nayf pranced around her, tickling her and sticking out his tongue, something surfaced in May's features, like fear or dismay: something terribly sad yet, at the same time, spiteful and quite merciless.

306. I've forgotten the neighborhood we were in, the name of the madwoman whose house we left, the identity of the two friends and even how Nayf looked, but in this moment I can recall the girl's face as though I'd seen it just an hour ago. A little later when the rain was falling harder, Nayf started having a real go at her, panting: "May's family have left her! May's family have left her!" And the expression on her face remained unchanged as she replied, "Bless your heart! And where's your family then?" And we broke out laughing, not noticing till afterwards that without giving a single sign or warning Nayf

had sprinted off. And by the time we'd stopped laughing he was a scarcely perceptible dot moving away down the street that gleamed in the rain. That morning we learned for the first time that he had lost both his parents and an only sister who'd been about May's age in a car accident just a few weeks earlier.

307. This incident—or maybe May's face—brought us closer together than ever before. Two days later, Paulo and I sat conferring over Nayf and from what we said I saw that his disdain for life, his permanently maintained contempt, concealed a deep unhappiness and sense of loss. For his part, Paulo possessed a readiness or a desire for advancement that only later did I understand as rural. He never once admitted to the ambition that, more than most, moved him, intelligent though he was, and yet he yearned to lay the city open, to conquer it and to crush it in any way he could. And perhaps his subsequent anger at Nayf had something of jealousy in it, jealousy at a peer who'd bested him in this regard. As for myself, I was—more so than at any other time—given to watching things; my aim was to understand, and it seemed to me that this understanding would serve to put a distance between myself and life and maybe that's what allowed me to get on Saba's wavelength, to a degree not granted others. Given Nayf's death wish, given Paulo's calculating ambition, I'd no choice but to be prepared to look on from afar if we were to claim that broken egg from which we'd make the omelet of Secret Poetry.

308. One day, one month or less before the group's announcement, in the summer of 1997, Nayf came in with an illustrated book in English, a Nile crocodile gaping on its cover, and said: "Did you know crocodiles are the most ancient species on

the face of the planet? They're older than the dinosaurs." The teeth in the croc's cone-shaped muzzle were terrifying. Nayf explained that their only purpose was to slice up the prey; to digest its food—he said—the crocodile has to swallow gravel and stones and lie motionless in the sun. "Are you aware that crocodiles share all the characteristics of the secret poet, including an amphibious nature?" And when Paulo turned up Nayf opened the book and began translating for us, stressing those three attributes, the ones which led us agree to name ourselves, we secret poets, The Crocodiles: "The crocodile sheds thick tears as it devours its prey (the origin of the phrase 'crocodile tears'), the hide on its back contains a lattice of bone that makes it proof even against bullets, and unlike the traditional 'King of the Jungle,' it makes no display of its strength nor does it swagger about."

309. In his most celebrated work, Saqr Al Janaini depicts a literary group that rejects the very notion of the literary text: that finished article of whatever length, which has a beginning and an end and is written by a single individual. Saqr Al Janaini depicts a literary group from the nineties that rejects the notion that such a thing is possible, or desirable.

310. He depicts them as short story writers, thus sparing himself (here, as in his life) the headache that is poetry and the problem of defining it. Saqr has written texts that resemble poetry in every particular but is too fastidious to call them poems, and in his most celebrated work he depicts a literary group of young writers from the nineties whose members meet at some unspecified café near their homes in Haram Street to recite their scribblings or ad-lib new lines, interpolated with

theoretical explanations of the inspiration for their output (apprehended only afterwards); and they press on one another the injunction that nothing be completed.

311. He depicts them as being silent and withdrawn, until they start in on the recitations and debates and then it's endless screeching and squabbling and, as was the case with all such Nineties' wordfests, their screeching brings them no closer to any concrete thought nor even a feeling. But what Saqr is getting at with his group is that the unity or completeness of the text is a marsh light, that does not lead to the truth so much as place the figure of the author center stage: his person, or his words, or his treatment of reality, portrayed as more reliable than life itself, or set above it. What Saqr is trying to express, I mean, is that the truth's impossible.

312. The book in question, a short story collection entitled *The Incomplete Literature Group* was released by Merit Publishing in 2003, six whole years after our group was founded. Paulo and I shared the single copy he'd pinched from Merit's bookshop, from under the nose of its proprietor Mahmoud Hisham, as he always did with new books. The first story was the one that gave the collection its title; until I stopped seeing him for good, at the end of 2004, the conviction that this story was a reworking of The Crocodiles' own tale was the only thing I didn't disagree about with Paulo.

313. *Completed works are a narcotic*—Saqr depicted them as saying—*since what's completed is just the physical manifestation of the work; but as for that thing around which the body's woven, this is perpetually moving and transforming. We live now, by*

God's grace, in an age of abstract signifiers, each one a reference to
another. Understanding that the objective truth that should prop-
erly lie behind each signifier has disappeared, we may see that such
referral multiplies falsehood. Assertions of authenticity are founded
on error… People's use of the signifiers at their disposal to benefit
themselves is a swindle, because it's claiming ownership of what
cannot be owned. We are the ungraspable. No one shall ever hear
of us nor do we want to hear of anybody: we've left the shop. When
you read you cast your eyes over the author's ideas and set a value on
them: a check, and if it clears the reader grabs it up and takes it to the
shop of meanings, where he buys himself a meaning or two to adorn
the elegant mansions of his ego. Those golden dinars; those completed
meanings. But us, our dinars are forged: pure fakes. No different—
here's the point—*from the counterfeit merchandise in your shop.*

314. The Crocodiles' philosophy states that poetry, which in the
end is speech, must necessarily, and predominantly, overlap with
conventional usage, but that in order to be poetry it must also,
and necessarily, differ from such usage (hence Orhan Velli's
use of "strange"). Perhaps we were influenced by definitions of
the divine essence in Islamic scholasticism and the competing
accounts of the Quran's creation (which Paulo could bring to
our attention and explain, thanks to his Azharite education):
we were brave enough to admit, albeit a touch wryly, that poets
venerated poetry in the same way that Muslims venerated their
Book (and where we got the insight to perceive, with such radical clarity, that poetry was still venerated, and the courage to
profess it, I couldn't say). It wasn't a question of whether we
would venerate poetry—we'd decided we were poets and so we
venerated poetry—but rather of the approach we'd follow when
defining it, so that we might venerate it as it should be.

315. And we were brave enough to set poetry above every-thing. Like everybody else, with the difference that they denied doing it. And just as the Creator possesses eternal attributes that antedate His creation and are quite distinct from the far greater number of attributes He shares with His creations—this much we knew—so, too, poetry is set apart by an extremely limited number of attributes that it alone enjoys while holding a preponderance of attributes in common with standard usage (among the nonessential attributes poetry shares: musicality—including rhyme and meter—levels of meaning, allegory and metaphor).

316. The Crocodiles' philosophy states that poetry has only three essential attributes, which must be preserved if it is to be, or to remain as, poetry, to which Paulo later tried to add a fourth, relevancy—providing a possible justification for using tradi-tional publishing to reveal the secret and thereby contribute to history's recognition of the Secret Poet's true value—and which, we concluded, was logically incompatible with each of the first three. Which were: self-sufficiency (that it never be presented as poetry or published under that description, and if the reader were to recognize it as such, in a news report in some daily paper, in the margin of an old book, on an abandoned blog—and leaking poetry to such spaces was allowed though not enjoined—then that was the only way in which its poetic nature might appear); desire (that it not be written until the desire to write it came upon you; what I like to describe these days as joy: there's a joy that accompanies the arrival of poetry in one's head—no need to privilege inspiration over perspiration, but without the desire to write, poetry won't be poetry); inten-tion (that it be written with the intention to write poetry and

not some other text, literary or otherwise: in our view poetic intentionality was enough to ensure meaning and impact, and any definition that went further than this would only constrict creative potential).

317. I'm looking at a short manifesto penned by Laith Al Hayawan on the new poetics and I'm speechless. Confronted by this stuff, by its contradictions, I feel I'm from another planet. Not now, I should make clear, and not just me: in 1994—I feel—the three of us were from another planet; only today do I think that this—like our shared background, like our complete identification with poetry, let alone our writing of it—explains our bond and our ambiguous status within the circle.

318. I don't doubt for a moment Laith's good intentions, his striving to be accurate and fair, but what's this he's saying ... on your mother's religion, Paulo ... Nayf ... what is this Laith says about "the poet's prophetic gift," how it's an illness we were cured of in the nineties? And why does he imply that rhetoric—what rhetoric?—can never be more than a rash on the skin? What does it mean to say a poet can do without rhetoric? And what are poetics, anyway? How can you measure poetics or make appraisals on the basis that rhetoric plays no part in them? And leaving aside these difficulties—and while we're on the subject—I feel, confronted by this stuff, that Laith was the prophet; that no one was more suited to that than Laith.

319. Now, looking at the manifesto penned by Laith, I'm speechless at the extent to which it is a manifesto and ideological, at its laying down of laws, its negation of "the other." I'm speechless that its declared intention is to lighten the burden of

"the old" and promote diversity, but most of all I'm speechless that it gave none of us pause for thought when it was written. Looking back at the first decade of the new millennium, I can't believe that everything just carried on, so contradictory and stupid, right up until the last years of Laith's life. How standards went to shit since people wouldn't go outside the circle, preferring to substitute some other writer they called friend for a real reader—because any given number of writers on friendly terms will always, however much they deny it, become a group.

320. And though there was general consensus on the primacy of Wadih Saadeh and Sargon Boulos, not to mention Mohammed Al Maghout, over the noted free-verse poets (Paulo, Nayf and I had never heard of anyone except the noted free-verse poets) . . . in the nineties there was this idea about the self whose point I'm still unable to grasp: the self as the subject of the text, or as a value projected by its owner's public image as a kind of social worth that compensates for, or transcends, the worth of elegance and wealth. There was this idea about the self and another about awareness: that awareness is partial and relative, that it is peculiar to the individual; and that being subjective it is of necessity an error. An error both partial and involuntary, thus ruling out the possibility of interrogation, even in cases where the writing seems to contradict these qualities; and also (of course) justifying the maximum amount of ignorance: ignorance and idleness.

321. I look at the manifesto penned by Laith and I remember that individualism was a trend just as decamping to Alexandria became a trend and I remember that everyone was operating in the same "writing space" (as he called it). And despite extreme

hostility to the idea of the prophet-poet (as to that of the popular poet), no one let go of the idea that poetry was a form of discourse exalted above all, uniquely holy; and no one resigned from the social grouping that argued for the production of this discourse and promoted it, though—through the abstractions of Adonis and his followers—the prophetic status had morphed from inclusiveness and cohesion into a charming species of ugliness and vulgarity. For the first time I see with great clarity that there was never any real conception of difference.

322. Even here everything took place in a ghetto of monolithic purpose; how then did any talk of plurality and diversity ever get through to us? It goes without saying that every poet has his own take and tone of voice; goes without saying that texts aren't copied wholesale from one another (though that too would happen, later). But how did it ever occur to us that you, even as something in Egypt's history was opening up the job market, making money circulate a little while the government raked in the returns of privatization, that you could be an individual in the first place? What was it with us and slang? What made us say "I scratched it" for "I know," "dice-pair" for "group" and "scorched" for "mad" with a methodical pedantry that robbed the phrases of any possible freshness?

323. *It was your duty to liberate awareness before your fathers dragged it off to a room on the roof of some working-class tenement and strove to keep it there, imprisoned. It was up to you to slip into that room, creep up on awareness and make it fall in love with you, seduce it with the dazzle of particularity, the magnanimity of uniqueness, so that it would come with you. And so you did; you set its private parts astir with the promise of broader horizons beyond*

the airports. Not one of you sufficiently at ease with the others, your dreams too broad for the metal box of the microbus you all travelled in together; you all pitched in when the wheel fell off, helped roll it a pace or two, but that's all. And until you'd managed to entice awareness to some other place it was your duty to disown your names and wave flaming banners as you stampeded bare-assed down back alleys . . . until you'd turned your fathers into vice cops and your families into well-drilled anti-sniper units, more adept at hunting down the extinct creatures whose rotting stench still stains the pastures sprawling out behind the doorways. And before you mounted the podium to find that same stench seeping from friends of yours who play the part of a sovereign people, you'd taught yourself the vendors' cries to flog awareness through the street markets, waiting for an opening in a mall. You realized early on that your impudence could not go on with nothing to support, and that the thing you called love could take you to colder, more civilized climes; could learn you languages. Gradually the awareness became your own, though it was no less implicated in its imprisonment. In its dealings with plane seats, with the snows of squeaky-clean cities, it continued to operate according to the law of abduction and restraint. As though you were your fathers; as though, having succeeded in setting awareness free, you can find nowhere to put it but that same rooftop room where once it slept so peacefully so far from all this slander and abuse. (I don't recall which one of us wrote this, nor when.)

324. Of course there was a third idea as well, about transcendence. An idea of an equivalence between religion and morals and duty and, perhaps, sticking to one's principles (however straightforward the principle might be or innocent of theorizing); an idea that equated all these things and prohibited them absolutely. For generations to come the word "moral"

would remain, within intellectual circles, a gross insult. Belittling the value of such things to people—and parading the image of the punch-drunk poet in conflict with his taboos, something I sensed in Paulo himself when, following Millennium Eve, he punished Nayf for being so unforgiving over his relationship with Nargis—this belittlement, this parading, was an alternative to worship.

325. It occurs to me now, looking at the manifesto, that this idea of transcendence, especially among the rural members of the circle, contained a nauseating equivocation: you get the sense that the priority is not so much to change things as to keep them distorted or broken. Even as they'd defend their right to be atheists, you'd see them—and they'd never say they were atheists outright—playing up anything that might corroborate their heretical status and make them, in the eyes of wider society, heretical sons of whores. It would be another ten years before wider society so much as suspected that atheism—like demonstrating and sex and heavy metal, not to mention the rallying cry of Salafist Islam—was a civil right that must be claimed. So why was it, once wider society started to suspect, that no one tried to claim a single right?

326. And I remember that, back then, none of this had occurred to anyone. Even we hadn't been able to formulate it, save via the crooked path of secret poetry's philosophy; and we did not notice that through this formulation—as with Radwa Adel and the Third Communist Movement—we were, in actual fact, turning against the poetic slice of the circle, as it was then, in the nineties.

327. More than a decade on I look calmly at the manifesto and note that no one has transcended anything at all. And though the role of the man, and occasionally the woman, too, might be reversed due to mental illness (or with it as a pretext), men married women who cooked them food and women married men who found them jobs.

328. And more than a decade on—I recall—June 27, 2011, passed uneventfully: exactly thirty-five years since Nayf was born. I hadn't seen him since 2001. And it struck me that our parting had now lasted a decade on the dot. Today, writing from a place that would never occur to any living soul—no reason really why it should— why does it surprise me that I'm no longer able to summon up the features of my friend? I peer at the title of the activist's book as I try and fail to recall Nayf's face. I leaf through dictionaries until I find that the root of *mabsour*, "premature," is a synonym for haste: that a date palm that's *mabsoura* has been pollinated early, out of season; that anything *mabsour* has taken place before its time ... plucked green, rushed, pushed up to the starting gate too soon.

329. For Radwa Adel, the premature are those whose cycle begins or ends before they are ready, like a newborn that has to be placed in an incubator or fruit picked green. It's no trumped-up metaphor, especially if we take into consideration the phrase's clumsiness, the strange way it falls on the ears. I mean the title's not a happy accident: aside from the fact that it fits us three like a glove, it seems to me to describe the tragedy of Nayf with appalling precision.

330. When I learn of the existence of a translator of Ginsberg called Sargon Boulos I will not compare his translations with

those of Nayf; I'll make no effort to prefer one poet over the other. All I'll do is read: *One came who speaks, and another who is silent*. The most beautiful thing about the sentence is its suggestion that there's no difference. I'm the one who speaks but this doesn't mean there's any difference between myself and Nayf, who will be silent forever.

331. The Crocodiles' one insight was to appreciate the truth of the role that poetry played on the eve of the third millennium: that it was closest to a secret unspoken, or to silence. Perhaps I am a traitor, in the sense that I've decided to speak, but with a decade and a half gone by I believe that speech and silence have become one. When that happens there's only tricks of memory and conflicting stories. There's magic to mystery for sure, but when all is revealed nothing remains save interpretation. And interpretation depends on things hanging together and this, by its nature, is eroded with the passing of time and passed-down stories. What remains is neither clear nor obscure. It's a soup. A strong-smelling soup in which, you feel, you're floundering, holding your head just above the surface so as not to drown. It's not important which of us is swimming in this soup; what matters is that it's one person and that he has actually gone under, or nearly so.

332. And whether as the man drowning in the soup or as something else, I imagine the activist's last steps towards death, lizard-slow, though the whole thing can only have taken seconds; as if I'm using the years that separate me from the last scene in the life of Radwa Adel to pad it out: fourteen years I've had—at my leisure—to stretch out the span that contains each and every split second of her suicide. I do this, perhaps, because

deep down I'm certain that what we suffered through from that day on was just the drawn-out dramatization, life-size, of things that happened on a microscopic scale to the activist during those last moments, and I'm aware that the suffering didn't peak for another four years; to be exact, that crowded period from July to November 2001. Myself, I played no part to speak of in the events of this period, but they obsessed me. And have done ever since, as I scrutinize our stance on suicide.

333. Maher Abdel Aziz said to me that Radwa Adel was the flower of her generation.

334. The times this thing has really forced itself upon me I've thought of looking up the forensic report on Radwa Adel and trying to work out exactly what happened. I never did and I never asked about her relative's address or put the scene as it took shape in my head to the test; not through laziness or a preference for gossip over hard facts—traits I don't deny I've inherited from the circle—but because such things will not bring back a cat run down by a car tire at dawn. Now, with the blood gone from the ground, indeed, with the road resurfaced to leave nothing of the accident behind, no ghostly trace, the fact still remains that the cat was run down, that it was shattered, flattened, glued to the asphalt; had it died instantly that would have been better by far, even if its body had remained in the middle of the road till morning, till the street cleaners took it away with the trash.

335. Some of my curiosity, I confess, revolves around what happened to Radwa Adel's body when she jumped: whether her head split open or her bones burst from her flesh; which sec-

tion of her innards were laid bare, exposed to view swimming in blood. And for a reason that may have something to do with the malevolence she directed at her struggle comrades in *The Premature: Portraits from a Life in the Student Movement* (published in the winter of the year she killed herself, while her other writings were collected and released the following summer), it pleases me to picture her brain having wholly broken free from the crushed skull and rolled intact against the curb. And when I do, I see the face, with no cranium behind, stretched out over jawbones, chin, what's left of forehead, come to rest in a such a way as to allow now-widened eyes a glimpse at the organ within whose folds and wrinkles took place everything we'd later play out: the giant walnut hidden in Radwa Adel's head.

336. Mojab Harb said to me: "We hardly slept for stories. It's true that when she told you about the relationships between party members you'd feel like throwing up, but it was enjoyable listening to even these stories, because of the pleasure of conversing with Radwa, and her lightness. And so we hardly slept for stories. Occasionally she'd rebel against this unforgiving way of dealing with the world. For moments at a time she'd reject it outright and then you could glimpse her desire to be like everybody else. When she laughed or sang, was pottering happily round the house, you sensed she'd caught sight of another life, one she craved but did not know how to reach. The problem was that she believed in honor but had no idea how to attain it outside suicide. She believed in honor and in a deeply complex way understood just how problematic and selfish it was. And as a woman this unleashed a feeling of impotence and she would turn on the person nearest to her: as though you were responsible for it; as though you, by expecting her to just get on and

live her life, had put your finger on her weak spot and exposed it. The respect they all showed her stemmed from her suicidal nature and their knowledge that she was quite capable of dissecting them with unmatched acuity and coldness. No one ever saw her humanity."

337. He said: "We scarcely slept. The stories. But you can't imagine how alone Radwa was, in spite of all those people who talked about her after she died. At bottom, I believe, her Marxism was an existential yearning for a father, hence—perhaps—her hang-up with Abdel Nasser. There was this scene in *Forrest Gump* where one of the characters flings mud at her father's old house. We watched the film together. During the scene I sensed Radwa stiffen and when I glanced over she was genuinely affected. That was one of her metaphors. And this was why I loved her—not because she suffered or made mistakes, not for her honesty or lies, but for something else, something I don't know how to say. Her lightness . . . She had this photo of herself in high school under a glass plate on the sideboard in the kitchen. I loved that photo and the character it showed; sometimes I'd dream of meeting that girl in some other country. You can't imagine how pleasurable it was to talk."

338. I've had over a year now—while I imagine her brain by the curb—asking myself how it was that we weren't interested in Radwa's Adel's suicide when it happened. It wasn't that it happened at the same time as our celebration of the founding of The Crocodiles, especially since we'd heard the activist's name and knew enough about her for it to ring a bell; we had friends in common, or acquaintances. There can be no doubt that we learned of her death when she died, as evidenced by the conver-

sation that took place between myself and Nayf on June 23, 1997, on the way to Opera Square. And yet . . . so many things bubble up in my head concerning those four years, which began in 1997 and were divided so absolutely from what came after 2001. And nothing clear amidst the bubbling: was Radwa Adel an important influence on the secret poetry movement? Was secret poetry representative of literary movements in the nineties? Was Nayf a convincing choice as the founding member of the group?

339. What is certain is that the group was formed the day of Nayf's birthday and the Radwa Adel suicide; is that Paulo bet Nayf that Nargis would divorce her husband before January 1, 2000; is that we, by founding the group, and though our philosophy constituted a break with it, had in fact officially joined the ranks of the intellectuals' circle or family: that entity both further-flung and deeper-rooted than any single class to which we might claim membership, but which, so far as society was concerned, did not exist at all. The activists, the writers, the great thinkers, they were the same as all those who had turned their backs on the traditional categories—whether members of some nineties group or as so-called "individuals" who refused to be categorized at all. Despite the differences, the declarations of individuality and individualism, we all of us—those and them—defined ourselves by reference to the circle.

340. Sometimes, it strikes me that the intellectuals' circle in Cairo is a perfect archetype in the Platonic sense, that like God or Satan its existence antedates the universe and will remain after Earth has crumbled away. In which case it's absurd to try and describe The Crocodiles' precise position relative to the circle, except to say that we, like others and to varying extents,

became it; which is what gives me the courage to say "our circle" when I mean no more than our group, and likewise allows me to occasionally ignore the distinction between The Crocodiles and other heirs of the Student Movement, and those from within the circle itself who just assumed it as their birthright.

341. In the mid-nineties we were around twenty years old, but we had friends ten or twenty years older and age was never a factor in loyalties that we'd discover with great suffering did not just fluctuate but were also—in fact, most of the time—fake.

342. Of course, there's another story here: the story of a person who left the apartment in Suleiman Gowhar a year before his father's death. Not all of it happened to him, perhaps, or perhaps it happened alongside things that were, at one and the same time, both more significant and pettier: things closer to the lies of The Crocodiles than to what they call life. Maybe this person graduated and got a job in journalism. Maybe he married. Maybe he divorced and failed to shoulder the burden of kids he'd fathered in his marriage like a sleepwalker. A person, say, who was living in Manyal when the thing they call The Revolution started up in 2011 and who, let's say, fell in love (and more than once). There's a story here. Over the seventeen years of its unfolding he realized that nothing in it concerned him in the slightest, that the things that did concern him were few and far removed from marriage and fatherhood and work, though they all happened in the same space and span, and were almost without exception connected to The Crocodiles.

343. In the mid-nineties we were around twenty years old and were it not for the circle—this is what I now see—we wouldn't

have found the thing that bound us together and took the weight, not of our writing so much as of our foolishness and the cost of our writing: the disappointments which kept us company and stemmed from each of us having avoided the life laid out before us—even Nayf, our sole success story—and that we justified (the disappointments, I mean) by saying that we wrote, or that we were intellectuals. In 1998 we read Ahmed Yamani's words: *No one can contemplate returning to house or hearth, though all he may rightfully hope for is for his own small patch of pavement and people who value the afflictions of lovers.* And from that day forth I've known that we'd stay out there on the pavements, no matter how hard we searched for a home.

344. "The Holm Oak" (one of my poems, written during Nayf's relationship with Moon): *The holm oak that should be blooming behind my shoulder / and that I can't see even in my dreams; / I do not know what a holm oak means; / For an instant, I think, I glimpsed it / between the blue sky's void / and the gray soil once a root, / the soil that was a root before the wheels pulped it / carpeting the floors of our lives as far as the eye can see; / I glimpsed it as I tracked a line through the car horns' paste, / like every day, unable to foretell the needle's turn; / It was dreadful, mythically beautiful; / mythically beautiful, truly, as is only proper / to a song-tree.*

345. 2001 was the year of breakdowns, global events aside. And while the writer Mustafa Zikri stayed holed up in Helwan, a flaccid boulder, reading twentieth-century classics and crafting heart-stopping sentences of pointless precision, people had started to emigrate—from the mid-nineties on, by study grant or marriage contract: Saqr Al Janaini to Germany, Wael Ragab to France. And now, with Al Yamani gone off to Spain, it seems

as though the world in which our group was born is become no more than a corpse.

346. Over the same period, those who died, died, those who left the cafés, left, and those who went mad, went mad or rediscovered Islam in the guise of Salafism. And because these transformations were really very difficult . . . These transformations were all difficult but the most difficult thing of all was that we (who'd learned how Nayf had been orphaned five years earlier) had witnessed the cat being flattened by the car's wheel, and the road deserted. We watched it living and we watched its flattening, then we watched it expiring, glued to the asphalt as the sun dawned, until it died.

347. That was Millennium Eve, on our way back from the party at the pyramids, not a week gone by since Paulo bowed to reality and admitted that he had lost the bet before the deadline set. He gave in, with overdone indifference and a bottled rage that would be directed, in its entirety, at the winner—Nayf—and more particularly at his love life: at Moon.

348. A week or less before Millennium Eve Paulo asked me to go with him to visit Nayf—at the time Nayf was staying at the house of his boss, who was away in America—so we met up at the Metro station, Paulo carrying a white cardboard envelope which he treated as if it contained some smuggled antiquity or a revolver. He looked deathly, defeated, something I noticed—strangely enough—not by an increase of irritation in his face but by its absence. Irritation was the default state of Paulo's face. And I guessed this had something to do with Nargis, though I hadn't the balls to imagine what the envelope contained, until

Paulo opened it before us both and said, addressing himself to Nayf: "Take it, you crazy bastard. You were right." For the briefest instant—Nayf and I appalled at what appeared before us in black and white, a strip of swaddled negatives underneath—it looked like Paulo might cry, but he burst out laughing, then pulled a packet of weed from his pocket as he crooned a smutty song. I remember that Nayf seemed genuinely sad as he slapped palm on palm, leaving the artist's genitals framed upon the table: "You bought your own bullshit about the bet. I was stating my point of view, that's all. It's you that bought your own bullshit, Paulo."

349. In their last meeting together—so I'd discover following our visit to Nayf—Paulo told Nargis some harsh truths. He said that when he looked at her after four years filled with the sound of her voice he saw nothing but a hollow pot with a skin stretched over its open mouth that could be beaten to make a noise, its tone and pitch determined by the whim of any passing drummer; that the circumstances of her upbringing in Minya and the problems it brought with it were not badges of honor or excuses; that she could have a poor and rural background and still not trade on some saga of struggle. And he said that she would not and could not divorce because the family Ashraf maintained was her only link to her son: the moment the family fell apart the act she'd put on to fool herself and others—that she was a mother, that she knew anything about motherhood— would be exposed.

350. "And then the truth will be more than you can bear, because you're a coward." Paulo to Nargis: "You turned the person who's put up with your shit and made a decent human being of you

into a cuckold, forced him to become a mother and housewife while you've kept on unchanged: a cunt in the worst sense of the word."

351. And in the same meeting, he said harsher things still against himself: that Nargis had spent four years scaring him with the idea that their love might give her a nervous breakdown and that he mustn't push her to take any critical decisions—if you leave me, she'd insist, my heart would be broken for ever—while the reality was that she never so much as considered altering her life for his sake and so ended up breaking his heart; that he should've believed her the day she said she wished that she were someone else and that he loved that person, not her; that he almost vomited whenever he remembered he was waiting for her.

352. Nayf grew comfortable with the lion. Not comfortable exactly, but used to its presence. Gradually, in the wake of his infatuation with Moon, he learned to sit with it in silence and gaze into its sad eyes. The lion itself no longer appeared as frequently as before—its visits grew further apart until September 2001, when they increased alarmingly—and though Nayf had not rid himself of the panicked sense that he was teetering on the brink of some unexampled madness, he'd begun to regard the lion as just an omen of an approaching moment beyond which there was no return. He was seized by the suspicion that his growing dependence on Moon—which he was unable to hold in check despite the nihilism that had driven him his whole life—was the true manifestation of this moment, that the lion was harmless in itself, and that his life falling apart before his eyes—like the beauty scattering from Moon's face

when she gave her sour and ugly grin—would have happened with or without the lion.

353. Nayf grew comfortable with the lion and surrendered, more and more, to his love for Moon, to his painful desire to possess her or remake her for his own sake. He had learned from her—having tied her hands and feet to the bedposts and striped her stomach with his belt—that the chalet where she stayed was on the coast, two hundred and thirty-two kilometers from Alexandria. In the first week of September 2001, and before it disappeared for good the following week, the lion had started to appear with alarming frequency. But all Nayf's panic was now centered on the impossibility of controlling Moon. More than once he thought of complaining to the lion, of turning to it, of asking it for help, but, recoiling from the lunacy of talking to a mythical beast that materialized inexplicably in his home, would back down at the last moment. On the morning of Tuesday, September 11, 2001, when he decided not to go to work as usual and set off in his car for the Desert Road heading for Kilo 232—when he pulled in at a gas station to fill the tank and check the tires and water—he was in the grip of a desire to burst in on her that had been gathering for ten whole days, ten days in which he'd managed to keep calm by telling himself stuff like she'd be back in a day or two. But in the early morning, having stayed up through the night of September 10, he found himself unable to resist.

354. From her he had learned the location of the chalet, where he headed in the early morning though she had been in Cairo since the tenth; she'd been in Cairo and hadn't told him. September 10: the day on which I met with Moon by chance in

Zamalek and took her back to where I lived, with her not leaving till late on September 11. It was three days before I heard what happened to Nayf, when Paulo found out from Shylock, who'd tracked him through his friends in the police after failing to find him at home; and by luck, good or bad, Moon wasn't with me; not then and not when I heard about the twin towers falling. She never spoke to me after that encounter of ours, nor to Paulo. For a long while afterwards I forbore from calling her and when I did the number had been changed. It's not certain, therefore, that Moon ever learned of Nayf's fate; we just speculated that it was one of the reasons for her disappearance. And she must have learned—if not trying to call or visit him in the days that followed, then from an acquaintance.

355. *Eaten by a lion in a bookstore on Cosmic Campus, starved by Professor Kandisky*—so Nayf would go on with the translation of "The Lion for Real," searching for the sense behind the words and nothing more—*I die in a vagrants' shelter inside a circus for lions. I wake up mornings and he's still there on my apartment floor, dying. "Terrible Presence!" I cried: "Devour me or die!" At that, that afternoon, he got up and walked to the door, resting his paw on the south wall to stop the trembling in his body. And from the highest height, the most fathomless depths, came a cry that shook the heart and thundered from my floor to the heavens, heavier than a Mexican volcano. He opened the door with a single shove and in a voice like gravel spoke: "This time, no, but I'll be back my little one, in time." O lion that's eaten my mind for ten years now and knows only hunger. The bliss of your contentment, O heavenly roar, why am I chosen? I believed your promise in this life and am ready to die. Long have I worshipped your ancient starved presence O God. I am in my room, awaiting your mercy. (End)*

356. By Millennium Eve not a week had gone by since I'd been cured of my love for Saba—the rights activist with whom Paulo had a fling four years before; I'd met her in October 1999 and she expressed great admiration for a text of mine she'd read from an old issue of the *Cairo* magazine, dating from the days Effat Yassin was managing editor there—just another woman from our circle in the foothills of her forties.

357. By Millennium Eve I'd been cured of my love but not quite cured of the memory of Giuseppe, her Italian husband, looming over me in the hallway of their house, while she was inside, going to pieces, persuaded that she'd lost her hold on me. Just like that the husband rebuked me for what he called my lack of feeling towards his wife, stressing that she'd supported me as a young writer while I'd been lapping up the free sex on offer. I was stunned that he knew about the sex (which wasn't exactly sex), having been used to hanging out with him on the basis that what was happening, was happening behind his back and that such deception was an ineluctable dictate of love. I didn't immediately grasp that my greater astonishment was at his siding with her against me, without the slightest embarrassment or sense of humiliation.

358. When Saba got serious about me, and her calls and our meetings were coming thick and fast, it never occurred to me that what was happening was quite routine; as I've mentioned, it was only later I learned even about her relationship with Paulo, and for a while there I assumed her interest in me was genuinely innocent ... until she confessed her love one golden evening at a Thai restaurant in Maadi, as we talked about the American poetess and suicide, Sylvia Plath.

359. When Saba came clean about her love, she seemed to me more poised than she ought to be at such a moment, yet the first time we were alone together in her house—I was perched on a high table in the dark—she squeezed her tall body between my thighs and clung to my head, weeping; and while I stroked her short, unkempt mop of hair, she made a quarter-turn till she faced the window where that same golden evening shone and did not light the room. She said, raising her palms and unfurling them like someone trying to stop something that's heading straight towards them: "I want someone to gather my scattered parts." I believed I was that someone, instantly. And despite the theatricality of the scene, despite many things, I loved her.

360. When Saba got serious about me I failed to notice. And until she confessed to me that her love life had begun with a childhood friend of hers—each adored the other and together they discovered the hidden pleasures of their bodies with no need for a third party, nor for men; but while her friend was following the dictates of a body that had urged her on since puberty, and stuck to the lesbianism she'd chosen for the remainder of her life (she, too—the friend—was well known in the circle), Saba never gave in to the truth . . . and when she broke her friend's heart, swinging aboard a more tractable sexual identity, it was not because her body led her to men—I would listen as she told me about her depression, the repeated suicide attempts before her marriage to Giuseppe, the over-riding importance of this Italian journalist who'd been resident in Cairo for twelve years when they married: the only one who understood and, in the end, forgave.

361. Gradually, I realized that the greater part of Saba's life revolved around a game that involved her implying she'd promised a man her body in exchange for an abnormal degree of attentiveness, then complaining that he was molesting her or trying to rape her when confronted by the expectations that came with his exertions. It hurt me to see her behave like this with others, especially those I knew, but I'd get past the pain when we shared a laugh or embraced; I told myself Saba was too mature, too wonderful for this game of hers to be intentional; that people really got her wrong and treated her, despite her innocence, with no respect.

362. For a whole year, while I played the role of family friend, eating, drinking, coming along on trips, without it once occurring to me that this affection was being entered on the balance sheet and that later I'd pay the price of the hospitality, while I helped Saba with her work and did her favors, I kept waiting for her to give me her body. She didn't. She didn't deny herself the pleasure of coming via fingers and tongue (just her coming, alone), but the mutual fondling stopped at a set limit beyond which she was paralyzed by feelings of guilt and anxiety, just like a teenage girl who has a relationship with a man for the first time in her life and so betrays her best friend who secretly adores her, for the sake of something that's legitimate, if not openly stated.

363. Saba was famous in the circle and people welcomed her presence as an agreeable poster girl for the non traditional woman, particularly as she enjoyed gossip and had no kids. Given the nature of her work, which brought her into contact with a complex web of relationships, which she hungered after

and whose pressure she complained of in equal measure, she had a lot to say about the rights of women and man's exploitation of the same: it was imperative she be liberated from the yoke of male hatred. And people, in effect, would applaud.

364. From my hypothetical vantage point in a future that dangled before us, unperceived, it seems to me that this was purest nonsense. Nonsense because—among other reasons—if you kept track of Saba, from 1990 to 2010 at the very least, you would know that what happened with me happened in its entirety, or nearly so, with all the Nineties writers, one by one (always for love and always with the promise of full intercourse left unfulfilled because something stopped her in her tracks at the critical moment), as well as with journalists and artists and others, among them the shining lights of a younger generation of writers; Nayf alone had nothing to do with her since he was already hung up on Moon by the time they met, but not because she didn't notice him and not because he was immune to her charms.

365. By Millennium Eve, if only half-consciously, I knew. I knew our bodies guide us, reveal our secrets to us and dictate our truest identity, that this was their gift even after they've grown corrupt or old. Now, as Nayf straightens up the car following the flattening of the asphalt fish—the pale puss—it's evident to me that there are people in the world who can't be guided by their bodies no matter how much they press them into service or use them to entangle others in their lives, and this, it seems to me, is the greatest tragedy of all. I mention this story because the sight of Nayf whimpering tearlessly in the driver's seat, while I thought of my lover that I no longer loved, was truly iconic.

366. Today it occurs to me that this rights activist saw all our private parts: an entire generation of poets exposed their sexual organs, and by necessity something of their hearts, to one not particularly beautiful woman who rarely let one of these organs disappear inside her because deep down it was women's bits she liked. This occurs to me for the first time in ten years and I laugh, die laughing, feeling something that is like grief but which is so unspoiled and stirred with yearning that I hold on to it after the laughter stops.

367. I tell these stories now to understand the revolution, but what terrifies me most is the thought that this is all there is, that each one of us has a story, more or less tragic, whose birth coincides with our dawning awareness of our bodies. A story that will repeat itself until we die—time after time after time: that you opted to go with the more tractable sexual orientation and feel nothing but guilt for abandoning the one you loved, or that some desire you felt forced you to withstand cruel self-examination in the mirror, and you with no idea what to do with it—and with the passing of years and people it becomes clear you didn't love or hate, so much as exploit others according to their readiness to make your story a reality, because their story could hitch a ride with yours, for a while. What terrifies me most is that this exploitation is all there is.

368. By Millennium Eve, if only half-consciously, I was aware that there was one thing in this world more valuable than everything else and that it was either an empty story (as it might appear while it was taking place) or a unique and unmatched truth; that it was more valuable, not only than ambition and achievement, but writing itself. Yet I knew that having this

thing, if only fleetingly, depended on your willingness to accord it value. You prized it, gambling that the other party didn't prize it half as much, and when they held it sufficiently cheap you let it go; the best you could do was to cultivate your burgeoning ill-will towards the one who'd wrecked your faith in it, this story, this truth that gave meaning to your life, however hollow and trivial.

369. To this day, I feel that this thing is irreplaceable, however much evil it might produce—sometimes I think that I've spent half my life searching for it and the other half mourning its loss; it's unclear whether I lost it every time because I too was urged on by an empty story that prevented me from prizing it, or because I only found it within the circle—but my rights activist, from before we met, was not prepared to do it any kind of justice.

370. Tonight the time will pass in thinking on Nayf and Paulo. On Paulo more than Nayf. And when I recall his sadness at Nargis's actions, when I recall his tears, not at their parting ways in late 1999, but from pure joy as he told her story at the start of 1996, I find great difficulty in producing an excuse for that groundbreaking artist whom I never met save once or twice. And though I knew from him that Nargis was at times sincere, that sometimes Nargis told the truth (and if she never gave the bare minimum expected of any mother in any culture in the world, what would make her give of herself for the sake of a man she loved?), because the truth was sad and painful and because it was she who was telling it, it was easier just to believe. Only lies let Paulo cling to the story.

371. In a subsequent session, before that same piece of blond hash had run out, Paulo would confess to me that he, even as he confronted Nargis with those harsh truths in their last meeting, was ready to go on loving her. Even with her ugliness so clear in his mind and in exchange for concessions which, it was equally clear, he would find monstrous and painful, he still believed he could win his bet with Nayf. What caused him to accept defeat was the discovery—after four years of haggling over things that by rights should never be haggled over, four years of finding excuses and inventing explanations—that Nargis was still negotiating.

372. "Until this moment," she told him, waiting for the reaction, "I saw a future for us together! Can't you see I came to Cairo for you?" She was waiting for a reaction, a retreat or an apology; he knew her words meant no more than that. "How many times must I tell you that practically speaking I'm divorced? And what do you expect me to do about my son if you can't help me take care of him? It's only now that the light's gone out, Paulo, because you've shown me that you can't forgive; only now, after all your hurtful words, do I see that I can't be with you."

373. And he would confess to me that only after these words were spoken and not a second earlier, was he sure that he had lost the bet.

374. By Millennium Eve I'd been cured. But over the course of a year and a half, till Nayf's story came to an end and distracted me from all worldly concerns, I would discover that when you love someone you define yourself by their existence and quitting them becomes a quitting of yourself: you must seize on some

essential part of your sense of self to pass through the crisis; you must reshape yourself somehow, a process that needs time, huge effort, and a parting; a parting, at least at first, is absolutely essential. Was it the parting Saba meant or the impossibility of unconditional sympathy when she spoke with such undue zeal about the yoke of male hatred?

375. And so, and because I went through hell redefining myself while the events in Nayf's story with Moon followed one upon the other, my account of their affair is most likely more intense and emotional than Nayf's own experience of it. In the period that ran from the falling-out with Nayf that led to our parting up to the end of everything—about six weeks, from July to September 2001—I thought of what the free-verse pioneer Salah Abdel Sabour had written, that *love, like poetry, is an unsuspected birth*; and I thought, as thousands must have done before me, that what love and poetry have in common, what drives them on, and maybe life in general, too, is joy. I don't mean happiness, or delight, or even that repletion that achievement brings. I don't mean the moment of mass hysteria we all experienced unexpectedly, in 2011.

376. What I mean is the moment you become aware of the mutual desire called love, or the moment a poem or passage arrives in your mind: both are governed—first and foremost—by another kind of sensation altogether, a joy whose most important characteristic is perhaps that it does not abide, and yet the memory of it does, to teach people and inform them of the place in which they are able to change, the place that can make them into other people altogether. One of the more brutal truths is that when love's gone we forget the joy. And

when we anticipate it, when we scan the horizon in vain, we lack the joy required to receive it. Then the world drops it in our path and we know it only by the joy we feel and we only cherish it to keep it with us. Months or years down the road, as it goes on or (more likely) after it has ended, we discover that we've become other than we were. And perhaps we surprise ourselves the day—as Sargon Boulos writes—*we cradle who we were in the arms of who we've become.*

377. Whether in writing or in contemplating life, if there be such a thing as poetry that differs radically from what is not poetry, then this thing, whatever else the case, must necessarily be greater and more precious than any person. If there be such a thing as poetry, then that thing is, to be exact, the joy of a poem's arrival. And that joy cannot be framed by some being with a body and a date of birth.

378. Is it because love's like poetry that I focus on love stories and so fulsomely retell them? In love stories, I believe, lies the secret of our prematurity, the seed of the thing that broke us before our time, that drained our batteries with no thought of responsibility to the nation. And a short while ago I had my hunch confirmed that political orientation and Marxist slogans were, for the Seventies Generation too, no more than a frail skin wrapped about a prematurity that would have happened in any case, exactly as with us.

379. My hunch was confirmed when I saw I understood *The Premature* far better once I substituted "idiot" for the words "intellectual" and "activist" wherever they appeared in the text. One example: "Those revolutionary idiots thought of themselves

as the vanguard of the Egyptian working classes." Another: "It is one of the ironies of Fate, or History if you prefer, that our generation of idiots are today descending one by one to the banqueting tables of nihilism." (Incidentally, what are these banqueting tables of nihilism supposed to be? And how do the people of a generation descend one by one?) This idiot idea's much clearer than setting down some other occupation, poorly defined and logically unrelated to the abstract theses and fraudulent formulations that ringed it round: intellectual, activist, Leftist; as though they were synonyms for whose meaning there was an established consensus—no ambiguity, no possibility of spin. Now I must find alternatives for "bourgeoisie" (haute and petite) for "people," "homeland," "revolution," for "class" too, for a not inconsiderable number of other words. Beyond a doubt, these alternatives will make it easier to understand the book.

380. In any case, after I finish reading, I shall return to the link between *The Premature* and *The Crocodiles*, and when I do the memories will press me to look closely at our failures; ours, the poets. Viewed like this, Nayf was the exception to the rule from the outset, which led many in the circle to resent him—if they weren't trying to exploit or hurt him—then to feel guilty later on . . . that is, when Nayf's story came to an end.

381. Sometimes, looking back over our debates and arguments and all the tangled paths that bound us till the bond was broken, it seems to me that failure was the only motivational force within the circle—was this why those of us who remained were later so hysterically covetous of jobs and family and stability?—and just as our forebears from the seventies, and the sixties before them, had prided themselves on being imprisoned

in the course of what they called political work, describing it as a defeat when such "work" was abruptly abandoned, as though it were some sly fart whose stench the new generations couldn't handle—that's what the activist called us in her book, by the way: "the new generations"—just like them, we felt pride in being unemployed and homeless, and especially in being lopped off the family tree, for we were country folk or from conservative backgrounds and our families couldn't handle our ideas.

382. The problem was that deep down we never accepted failure despite our realizing (some more than others) that success in this society was the opposite of what we wanted. And perhaps we'd never rid ourselves of our family's values as thoroughly as we'd assumed, of those values I recognized in the face of a doorman's one-eyed wife, split by a craven smile: the embodiment of whatever makes things like beggary, duplicity and prostitution a logic to live by. More exactly, having rid ourselves of these values, we found no functional alternatives and so we lived without values. And we weren't ready for that, weren't aware of how hard it was; what we'd shrugged off kept sneaking back to the place we hid our ambitions and there occupied a space that was like a confessional. And our need for such a space ate away inside us, where we kept our ambition hidden.

383. Today I've no doubt that the contradiction between our glorification of failure and our failure to accept failure—like the homes of nineties intellectuals left open to guests whose presence was never welcome—was the basis of the breakdowns that succeeded one another throughout 2001 and forced us, on an individual level, to change our lives.

384. In the spring of 2011, I recall—having moved some years before from Alexandria, where he'd worked his whole life as a secondary school teacher, to Kuwait—I met with Mojab Harb during the few days he spent in Cairo on his annual holiday and the talk and laughter brought us to the Nineties poets. Neither Radwa Adel nor The Crocodiles came up that night (I'm not sure if Mojab ever heard of our group); we grieved over nothing and nobody, just tackled the anxiety and madness of the circle head-on. I said that the revolution had opened the intellectuals' circle to society, and he said it would draw back the veil of dissent and difference that enveloped the circle to reveal that society itself lay within.

385. I met with Mojab and remembered how—how suddenly—we had grown up.

386. All of a sudden we grew up and our shyness, our exuberance and our fear, too, fell away, or one part of each of these things did. But the most monstrous thing was that we knew we'd grown and what showed we knew was that we noticed traits in our contemporaries, and maybe also in each other, that we'd never seen before. It seems strange to me now that the clearest sign we'd grown was when we noticed people agreeing with things they would otherwise have rejected on personal grounds, for instance, or voicing opinions not because they really held them but because they seemed like the right ones to hold.

387. Suddenly these people seemed like cannibals; and, like the Palestinian Authority, it seemed they traded on their problem more than they tried to solve it. We knew we had grown when

we noticed that they took refuge within the vast family that was our circle, huddling with their kind for warmth while treating one another as viciously as they did others. And we knew more surely when we started to suspect that they turned their backs on the mainstream, not because they hated it but because the margins were their means of entering it as conquerors, at their backs the long and rocky road that runs through Downtown's shabby cafés, from village to town. And when we'd grown we knew that even in poverty and insubordination, even in society's least serried ranks—the most *hilihli*, as they say of things left to their own devices, the most haphazard and natural—there was no private life. There were no personal relationships, however intimate and permanent the friendships seemed, because no one had any real relationship, other than with the circle.

388. In the spring of 2011 I met with Mojab. As I was saying when the grief struck. I don't know if I'm thankful for the file before me on the computer screen as it moves past one hundred pages. The desire to descend to the scene of events still evades me but the agony of my distress comes through more and more. Maybe I've really started to feel guilt; the pain in my stomach barely dimmed. I know none of those who've been killed, but it's as though you went to sleep and woke naked in the street. Is what we see truly all we have? Were The Crocodiles ever asked about what it was that folded Egypt into its embrace sixty years ago?

389. All of a sudden we grew up, between Paulo's separation from Nargis and Millennium Eve, twelve years before the day that someone else with links to Radwa Adel wrote me: "You need to understand where this Egyptian mentality comes from. Why is prostitution such a fundamental part of our lives,

like it's the ultimate solution beyond which there's only noth-
ingness? Why should malice be an acceptable alternative to
intelligence and ridicule replace fun? Why are people happier
to steal their pleasure than to delight in pleasure itself, like a
housemaid wearing her mistress's clothes on the sly? Why this
pleasure in stealing life, rather than living it? Why are we so
afraid of radical solutions?"

390. The strangest thing in my relationship with Mojab was
that whenever we talked I'd think of Nargis. With a line, like,
"people are happier to steal their pleasure than to delight in pleasure itself," for instance, I don't think of Radwa, I don't think of
Saba, nor of Nayf, nor Paulo, nor Moon, nor of The Crocodiles.
Only her, preserved in the memory of just one meeting at the
café alongside the Townhouse, amidst the car repair shops that
ring Maarouf Street, the café we called "Lipton" for the yellow
tea ads plastered on the plastic sheets that shade its seats the
length of the pavement, and which, post-2005, suddenly and
without warning, became known as "The Trellis." Why people
acquiesced to this name change I've never understood.

391. She appeared innocent—shy, the slight stammer in her
speech, for all that her unsure eyes were tainted by a trace of
hunger held in check—and may even, to the unobservant, have
seemed to be of aristocratic stock: her looking out at the waiters
and the panel-beaters on every side with a mix of sympathy and
condescension and them, tolerating her presence only as some
Westernized girl from another world, or as a foreigner.

392. Following my conversation with Mojab, I consider everything this look of hers demands.

393. We grew up and within a year, two, Nayf was driving his car faster and faster down the Desert Road and thinking of the lion. Of course, he was obsessed with Moon, as I imagine: impatient to meet her and dreaming up different scenarios as to where he'd find her boss, the one she stayed with, when they met—Lying down in his room? Sitting with her in the lounge? On top of her in bed? . . . But as is the case in all such charged and fateful moments, I imagine him thinking of something else, something other than that which immediately obsessed him: of the lion. That the lion had reappeared every single day through August, then vanished utterly in its last week; that Shylock was the sole witness to the lion's appearance and that he might well deny it if asked; and that for all these months no sound of any sort had come from the lion, nor smell.

394. This is how it happened, close enough, as broken down by Paulo and myself with the benefit of all the available evidence: at approximately half past one on the afternoon of September 11, Nayf was on a relatively deserted stretch of the Alexandria-Matrouh highway, between Kilos 25 and 75, driving at colossal speed despite the strain of seeing clearly through the heat and dust, and switching carelessly from lane to lane. Suddenly, at around quarter to two, the road started to fill up with trucks. Nayf managed to avoid hitting one that roared up on his right at some unpropitious moment, but the force with which he wrenched the wheel brought him out of his lane and, having clipped the truck's trailer, left the red Mazda momentarily planted in the dead center of the highway; following this abrupt check the car listed heavily but didn't overturn, only for a second truck coming up behind to smash into it, accelerating unawares and crushing the driver's side before it managed

to come to a stop. (And, as though sketching out a plot for some dreadful novel about 9/11, Paulo and I would calculate that the truck hit Nayf at a quarter to two, the same time as the first plane collided with one of the World Trade Center's twin towers in New York, though Nayf—as we learned from the medical examiner's report—did not die of bleeding on the brain and trauma to his lungs until approximately two o'clock, the time at which the second plane struck the second tower: three minutes past two, Egyptian time.)

395. This is exactly how it happened, as conjured up by me once I was certain—for some unknown reason—that Nayf really was thinking of the lion: at half past one—his eyes on the road—Nayf became aware of a rattling sigh inside the car and looked around to find, on the passenger seat, an old man he'd never seen before; just how he'd managed to slip into the car and when he'd slid up beside him was not clear in the slightest. It was at this point that his driving started to become erratic, leading, fifteen minutes later, to the accident that would claim his life. Naturally, there was nothing in the wreck besides his body. The old man sitting beside him was strikingly short with a disproportionally big head, his long hair matted like a lion's mane and yellowish, and his nose large and flat. When Nayf, having lost the power to speak or scream, peered into his face—the other silently and sadly gazing back—he noted with alarm that the old man's eyes were yellow. And just before the old man opened his mouth to make the sound that begets a nausea whose like no call of beast or machine din can match, no matter how loud or ugly, as Nayf was dodging the first truck, he said, still gazing at him with the same sad expression on his face: "You could have complained to me, my boy, but it's your destiny."

396. Ten years on or more from Nayf's death I've come to understand that evil begins when you disdain what you need: refusing pity when you deserve it, luxuriating in failure when you burn for success, setting your desires aside in favor of some social project, or seeing your desires as inimical to achievement. Perhaps disdain is one of the universal characteristics of the poet, though a line like this would have been enough to bring ugly mockery from our mouths: conventional representations of the poet made us genuinely angry. We went on warring against our buried ideas about ourselves and it never occurred to us for a moment that we might embrace parts of these selves instead, nor how weak and pathetic they were, how prone to leap from a balcony on the eleventh floor, or twelfth. By means most complicated we destabilized the customs we'd been raised to see as stable and refused to have anything to do with institutions that could not provide an income large enough to keep us satisfied nor a home as a home should be nor a lifestyle that would enable us to produce extraordinary things. Sincerely or falsely, we continued to call our relationships friendships—Friendship! How many the crimes committed in thy name!—and perhaps it was these very customs, their stability, that made us cling together tighter than we'd have done were circumstances more amenable.

397. Radwa Adel wrote insincere and ideological texts and many agree that they (the texts) deserve to be forgotten, yet Radwa Adel herself remains a suicide and it's as this that a slightly greater number of people still remembered her for the course of a generation or two. Remembered her in phrases like "the case of" or "the tragedy of," adding that she was an activist— an intellectual, writer, great thinker—one of the leading figures

of the Student Movement or the Seventies Generation. They might pronounce on the nature and failure of that generation, but they would never refer to what she wrote, to any concrete contribution she made in those areas associated with her name. What counts is that she drew attention to the family of intellectuals. And maybe we too, or one of us, will be remembered the same way. It might be said of Nayf, for instance, "He wrote poetry," and if the speaker were generous: "His poetry wasn't bad." But this would only ever be offered as a passing comment, while talk about what happened to Nayf on the personal level, would treat him as a case, or a tragedy.

398. Ten years on or more—with the Salafist Nour Party and the Freedom and Justice Party of the Muslim Brotherhood sweeping the parliamentary elections now under way, with security still murdering and plundering in the streets and with the MP units from our own armed forces dragging protesters along the ground, stripping off their clothes, beating them to death, then dragging their corpses to the rubbish dumps, aside, that is, from sniping them and torturing them in public buildings—I've come to know that evil begins when man imagines that he, by means of knowledge, creed or identity, can change the course of a life that's slipped from his shoulders, like a suitcase for which a net must be spread in the valley before he may sit inside it and arrive like that.

399. Ten years on—while from afar I follow the progress of a revolution we were waiting for not knowing that we waited and which, when it came, thundering through like the last train, left us shell-shocked on the platform—I think how all of us became a case or tragedy: if any memory should remain to us,

its gist shall always be the ignominies of love and death and birth. Did all this happen so that we might be a fitting subject for the gossip of a slightly greater number of people? I feel my body sinking in the soup as I wonder: All this?

400. Paulo and I held a wake for Nayf attended by many of those who'd turned up to the secret celebration of The Crocodiles' announcement at my family's apartment on Suleiman Gowhar in 1997. We held an *azza*, a mourning ceremony, in Paulo's apartment in Agouza, but Quran-free: more like a wake, where we drank coffee, smoked weed, discussed the attacks in New York, the anticipated American reprisals against Muslims, and the delight with which the greater part of the Egyptian people had met the scenes of destruction and death. We were shell-shocked, Paulo and I. We joined in the conversation but rarely and the weed did not affect us. For a week, a week spent glued together and periodically bursting into tears, we stayed silent. Our world had been transformed to a degree that would make it impossible for us to remain friends. Bin Laden's rise as a hero was in itself a sign that a whole lifetime had come to an end for another, and maybe a better one, to begin. With the execution of Saddam Hussein in 2006 and Obama's election as America's first black president in 2008 each of us became something distinct from the other. Paulo and I. And we were crocodiles no more. Was our grief over Nayf a grief for our group and for our friendship, too?

401. What's certain is the tasteless fact that Nayf finally died at Kilo 45 on the Matrouh Road as the second of the World Trade Center's towers was hit in Manhattan; and perhaps he died—at

two seconds past three minutes past nine, New York time—the precise instant it was hit.

402. What's certain is that he settled on the following version of Allen Ginsberg's poem exactly six weeks and four days before his death (the date of his last entry in the file of his PC into which he transcribed the poem from his notebook, was, as I discovered, the date of our last argument: July 7, 2001): *The Lion for Real – Be silent for my sake, O pensive god – I came home to find a lion in the front room / and sprinted to the stairwell crying: Lion! Lion! / The two secretaries next door: each tied back her dark hair and with a clap their window slammed shut / I hurried to the family home in Patterson and stayed two days // Called up my analyst, a student of Reich / who'd barred me from the sessions as a punishment for smoking hash / "It happened!" Thus, panting in his ear: "There's a lion in my front room" / "Unfortunately there's no room for discussion." He put down the phone // I went to my old boyfriend and we got drunk with his girlfriend / I kissed him and with a mad gleam in my eye announced I had a lion / It ended with us fighting on the floor. I cut his eyebrow with my teeth so he threw me out / and I spent the night in his jeep parked outside the house, masturbating, moaning "Lion!" // I found Joey my novelist friend and roared in his face: "Lion!" / He looked at me with interest and read me his spontaneous high-flown poetries written as the ignu writes [according to Ginsberg, the ignu is someone who lives once and for eternity and sleeps amid the family of other men] / I listened out for the lion; only heard the elephant, the Tiglon—offspring of tiger and lioness—Hippogriff, Unicorn, Ants / But knew he understood me when we fucked in Ignaz Wisdom's bathroom // The next day he sent me a note from his retreat in Smoky Mountain / "I love you Nunu and I love your delicate golden lions / but as there's no soul and no*

obstacle why then your dear father's zoo hath no lion / You told me your mother went mad before she died so expect no mythical beast from me for your bridegroom." // Confused and dazed, raised up above this life entire, I bethought me of the real lion starving mid his stink in Harlem / and opened the room's door to be met by the bomb blast of his anger / He roared hungrily at the plaster on the walls but nobody could hear him through the window / My eye caught the red edge of the neighboring apartment block standing in deafening stillness / and we held each other's gaze his implacable yellow eye at the center of a halo of red fur / My eye alone grew watery but he stopped roaring and bared a fang in greeting / and I turned to cook broccoli for supper on the iron gas stove / I boiled water and had a hot bath in the metal tub beneath the sink // He did not eat me and though I was sad that he was starving in my presence / by the following week the wasting had left him a sick rug full of bones, the wheat stalks of his hair falling out / his reddened eye malevolent as he lay aching his hairy head in lion palms / by the bookcase made of egg crates, filled with slim volumes of Plato and Buddha // I'd stay up next to him every night averting my eyes from his hungry moth-eaten face / and gave up eating myself, him weaker, roaring by night while the nightmares visited me: / eaten by a lion in the Cosmic Campus bookstore in Columbia University or as a lion, forbidden food by Professor Kandisky, dying in some filthy flophouse in the lion's circus / and I'd wake mornings with the lion still added to my presence dying on the floor before my eyes. "Terrible presence!" I cried: "Eat me or die!" // That afternoon it rose and walked to the door its paw against the south wall to hold its trembling body steady / let out a wounded creak that shook my heart from the roof of his bottomless mouth / and thundered up from my floor to heaven, heavier than a volcano in Mexico / He pushed the door to open it and in a gravelly voice said: "Not this time little one, but I'll be back again." // O Lion

that eats my mind for a decade now knowing naught but hunger /
not the paradise of Your contentment, O roar of the universe how
am I chosen / I have heard Your promise in this lower world and am
now ready to die / I served Your enduring starved presence, O Lord,
I am in my room awaiting Your mercy – Paris, 1958.

403. On January 28, 2011, after sundown in Qasr Al Aini
Street—the protesters already beating rocks against the lampposts, a call to arms the like of which you've never heard, the
street empty of cars and no pedestrians abroad aside from the
protesters, the security forces fallen back to Tahrir Square from
where they fire tear gas, birdshot, rubber bullets . . . the protesters have ripped out the metal barriers around the gas station
to fashion shields from behind which they pelt security with
Molotov cocktails brought up in soft drink crates and no sounds
but orders swapped back and forth between the demonstrators
and that unearthly alarum: what it's telling you, you don't know,
though you know it means something momentous is in the
air because before your very eyes you've seen one (more) killed
either by projectiles or because some vehicle with diplomatic
plates ran him down, then sped off into the distance; like a sign
of the apocalypse, the horizon black with smoke, and life as
you know it at a standstill: the sound of stones beating against
lampposts and protesters lugging bottles full of gas and shel-
tering behind metal shields in formations that take shape amid
a silent hysteria of rage—what's certain is that the protesters
on the front lines are all teenagers except one handsome Omar
Sharif look-alike in his mid-thirties, seen moving metal sheets
and organizing the front lines with great gusto. And more than
one intellectual to spot this man, who never appeared at any
protest before or after, swore he was the spit and image of an

obscure poet who'd died aged twenty-five on the north coast road. Afterwards, during what was known as the "Battle of the Camel" on February 2, 2011, when those who gave the orders in Egypt dispatched quantities of blade-wielding men—some on horse- and camel-back—to break the sit-in in the square, it was said that Gamal Mubarak, the president's son and anointed successor, pushed a plan to release the predators from their cages in the Giza Zoo (as convicted felons were let out to terrorize residential neighborhoods from the night of January 28) and herd them to Tahrir. The plan was never carried out, but someone said that at the height of the battle between the demonstrators and the thugs, who, beaten, fell back to leave the square to the snipers in the dark of night, they'd seen a lion roaring in fright and powerless to attack.

404. Now, as I sit outside it all, waiting for another revolution to be staged on January 25, 2012, and not believing in its worth, as I wait for God to appear again having forsaken even poetry, I think on Moon from where reports reach me and sense that the ultimate madness on whose brink Nayf teetered in 2001 has, ten years on, come to blight the whole land; and I feel that it—the very same—is the madness of Radwa Adel at the instant of her suicide. During that period in which it seemed that a spontaneous movement would eradicate the futility of living in Egyptian society, meaning really did return to words like people, homeland, revolution, even, perhaps, to bourgeoisie; and though this period did not last and though the meaning vanished again with its passing, it's been clear to me ever since that Radwa Adel really did kill herself for our sake. Without knowing it, she killed herself that meaning might return to words.

405. I am Youssef, Gear Knob, anyone you please: the founding member of the Group for Secret Egyptian Poetry. And what is certain is that with these words, written in a future that dangled down from the mid-nineties on, I end the first document in the file called Crocodiles.

THE REVOLUTION FOR REAL

Not the bliss of your satisfaction O roar of
the universe how am I chosen

—ALLEN GINSBERG, The Lion for Real

Back from Alexandria via Tanta to find the revolution beneath
    my bed
And bent double by the light of the bedside lamp, cheek level
    with the bed boards
I make out millions stampeding and defending themselves
    with stones, each one a butt end still aglow,
Lifting signs like stamps and carving slogans bigger than their
    bodies in the parquet; I eavesdrop on their cries.

A last glass of vodka not yet vaporized out my skull from a lay
    in Alexandria left undone,
Pissed bones popping as I fight back tears, shredding my
    clothes at the window:
The revolution's happened, you sons of whores! The
    revolution's here for real!

I'd left my girlfriend in Ibn Al Farid Street over the pickle
    place receiving the old guard, come to pay their respects,

And me missing neither lay nor sea nor her mother's face
    widowed just hours before,
Nor my dad, dead a decade back,
Nor a saint round the back of the Shrine café who numbers
    among his blessings a member bigger than a military
    policeman's truncheon,
But rather my ear, soaked in Azareeta because her tears were
    dripping from my phone.

I splash my clothes with red ink and rush to work to lie down
    at the boss's door
The revolution was not with workmates, nor on the Metro
    nor even in the throats of martyrs resurrected as Central
    Security hoods.
Drifting through the realms of Egypt Rail how come I
    couldn't catch it before it fled to my room?

Weak after a night in the office bathroom I whisper to the tea
    boy: Without revolution life's unbearable;
Do you know that Ibn Al Farid said a lover's death is life and
    better to kill than part forever?
Sadly, just as there's no change without slaughter there's no
    time without waiting;
Know the angels?
Angels? he asks scornfully, fingering a bald patch like a
    boulder and, gazing at me with pity, slips me five pounds

A lion with Moleskin I make for a lioness to let her know the
    revolution's not in Tahrir Square
And sipping a frappe on the back of a smoothie chasing three
    double espressos at a branch of Cilantro

I screech over my laptop screen at a teen Catholic: There's no
    such thing as penis envy!

From Doqqi to Tahrir many times over in the company of a
    young poet, from Tanta, too,
Knowing our efforts have been wasted when my girl, bereaved,
    don't answer,
And with Zizo keeping a Jordanian girl company the night I
    got her call, was her sudden misfortune the seal set on our
    compact?

When she answers at last I persuade my poet friend that
    there's a sit-in in my room, for real: We set out unarmed,
And he shifts along behind me on his knees, past the bedside
    table in Bermudas, a spy, a snooping plant
Crowds of protesters clustering around a stone cake: an old
    sole
Just like we were
Tanks, matchboxes and F-16s like pins, shameless demagogues,
By night, between the bed boards and the mattress: snipers

We hump the pillows after I tell my friend God's immanent
    in train tracks and the revolution will not be WiFied
I picture my girlfriend knelt before me in her black blouse, our
    heavenly grief as I come in her throat
And when mother wakes us in the morning I don't resist, I see
    the maid, her hoover with its Eagle emblem,
I see the national flag aflutter in alien hands and know that we
    shall not defeat Israel.
My friend's furious, sleepdust in his eye as the hoover's hose
    reaches beneath the bed;

When the soap and mops come out I warn him off the maid,
	with difficulty: No point raping her now!
Nothing but the hoover's drone while he weeps,
Nor blood nor iron,
The bedroom's parquet once more clean and clear,
And where books of poetry stood on the shelves, bottles of
	Dettol and bleach, sponges and embroidered cloths;
Suddenly my bed sighs to the siren's wail, the sheets catch fire,
	the mattress detonates,
Bedside table morphs to dread lion roaring my friend vanishes
	the writing on the walls:
A panther ejaculates every twenty minutes when it mates and its
	tongue is rougher than sandpaper.

My Bereaved Darling, Conferrer of the final orgasm: death
	knits our lives together;
I have seen the comers and goers, kissed bearded ones and run
	from hatchet men on Metro steps,
Have borne my saint down to the grave's gloom for your
	father's ease of mind and drowsed cross-legged between
	two carriages to Cairo,
Have found you beneath my bed and my mother's army in my
	room,
Have offered up my neck to the lion's mouth.

ABOUT THE AUTHOR

Novelist, reporter, poet and photographer Youssef Rakha was a reporter, copy editor, and cultural editor-cum-literary critic at *Al-Ahram Weekly*, the Cairo-based English-language newspaper, and the founding features writer at the Abu Dhabi-based daily, the *National*. His work has appeared in English in the *Daily Telegraph*, the *New York Times*, *Parnassus Aeon Magazine*, *McSweeney's*, and the *Kenyon Review*, among others. His photographs have been exhibited at the Goethe Institute in Cairo. Seven books by Rakha have appeared in Arabic. He was chosen among the thirty-nine writers representing the new voices of modern Arabic literature at the Hay Festival/Beirut World Book Capital competition, Beirut39 in 2009. His essay, "In Extremis: Literature and Revolution in Contemporary Cairo (An Oriental Essay in Seven Parts)" appeared in the Summer 2012 issue of the *Kenyon Review*.

ABOUT THE TRANSLATOR

Robin Moger is an Arabic translator currently living in Cape Town, South Africa. From 2001 to 2007 he lived in Egypt, where he worked variously as a journalist, translator and interpreter. He is the translator of two published novels, *A Dog With No Tail* (AUC Press, 2009) by Hamdi Abu Gollayel and Ahmed Mourad's *Vertigo* (Bloomsbury-Qatar Foundation Publishing, 2011), and is a regular contributor to *Banipal*, the magazine of modern Arab literature.He was principal translator of *Writing Revolution: Voices from Tunis to Damascus* (IB Tauris, 2012) (published in the US by Penguin as *Diaries of an Unfinished Revolution*), which won a 2013 English PEN award for Writing in Translation. His translation of Nael Eltoukhy's novel *Karantina: Seven Women Who Ruled the World* is due to be published by the American University in Cairo Press in 2014.

ABOUT SEVEN STORIES PRESS

Seven Stories Press is an independent book publisher based in New York City. We publish works of the imagination by such writers as Nelson Algren, Russell Banks, Octavia E. Butler, Ani DiFranco, Assia Djebar, Ariel Dorfman, Coco Fusco, Barry Gifford, Martha Long, Luis Negrón, Hwang Sok-yong, Lee Stringer, and Kurt Vonnegut, to name a few, together with political titles by voices of conscience, including Subhankar Banerjee, the Boston Women's Health Collective, Noam Chomsky, Angela Y. Davis, Human Rights Watch, Derrick Jensen, Ralph Nader, Loretta Napoleoni, Gary Null, Greg Palast, Project Censored, Barbara Seaman, Alice Walker, Gary Webb, and Howard Zinn, among many others. Seven Stories Press believes publishers have a special responsibility to defend free speech and human rights, and to celebrate the gifts of the human imagination, wherever we can. In 2012 we launched Triangle Square books for young readers with strong social justice and narrative components, telling personal stories of courage and commitment. For additional information, visit www.sevenstories.com.